I0551222

CLAIMING POWER

BOOK THREE OF THE FRIENDS & LOVERS SERIES

PE KAVANAGH

BOLD
SOUL
BOOKS

CLAIMING POWER

Copyright © 2018 Pascale Kavanagh

All rights reserved. No part of this book may be used or reproduced in any manner whatsoever without written permission except in the case of brief quotations embodied in critical articles and reviews.

This book is a work of fiction. Names, characters, places and incidents are either the product of the author's imagination or are used fictitiously, and any resemblance to actual persons, living or dead, events, or locales is entirely coincidental.

For information contact: Pascale Kavanagh www.pekavanagh.com

Cover designed by Olivia Pro Designs and Bliss Designs

E-book ISBN: 978-0-9994679-8-5

Paperback ISBN: 978-0-9994679-9-2

First Edition: September 2018

10 9 8 7 6 5 4 3 2 1

For those who stand against tyranny, corruption, and the sullying of the human spirit.

CHAPTER 1

Ten months to election day

*C*onnor squirmed in the wide leather seat, his patience stretching dangerously thin. Stanley, whose bug-eyed shiny face always expressed angry surprise, had hardly taken a breath between streams of expletives into his phone. Connor had been waiting for twenty minutes, but it didn't look like the rant was going to stop anytime soon. Mild restlessness was about to turn into full blown anxiety and all the deep breaths in the world weren't going to calm him down.

He could just step out of the car for a second, stretch his legs, move his body, clear his head. Stanley's rage would be directed toward him soon enough, complete with finger-pointing and name-calling, but he didn't need to sit there and wait for it. Connor reached for the door, Stanley grabbed his arm, and a vision of punching Stanley in the face—multiple times—froze them both in place. But just for a second.

A twist of the wrist freed Connor from the hold; a kick of the door freed him from the stifling space.

An indelicate slam of the door cut off the string of profanities coming from inside the sleek black Towncar. Connor broke into a familiar pattern of pacing and scanned the unkempt loading dock, so different than the stunning entrance of the building. Young people in chef uniforms hauled crates out of white panel trucks, while two men in suits barked orders. They'd arrived at the Mellon Auditorium, the location for his next event.

It surprised him when Stanley mentioned reserving the Mellon. Being the closest event space to the White House made it nearly impossible to book without the highest level connections. Clearly, Stanley had them. Maybe Uncle Robert had pulled a few strings as well.

Connor matched his breaths to each long stride. This was a big night, when his campaign for Senate would be taking the next step. He'd be asking people for money and votes. Asking them to trust him.

A burst of wind chilled his face, a cold sweat broken out across his forehead. What was he thinking? He wasn't ready for this. He was a small-town Mayor. Sure, he had a political legacy, and yes, he'd done great things for his community, but this... This was another league, entirely.

He nearly reached the caterer's van, turned and walked back toward the car. He paused at his reflection in the blackened windows and ran a hand over his hair. No reason, as his hair never got mussed. Just to make sure his head was still screwed on, maybe.

"Dad," he whispered. "I need your help, here. I might have gotten myself into something way over my head."

He didn't expect a response, considering his father had died three weeks before. But what he saw in the reflection looked more like his long-gone grandfather, the one the streets and buildings were named after. The one who'd terrorized his childhood.

"Grow a set! You're not just any boy," Grandad would say. "You're Connor Barrett. Eldest grandson of Virginia's most beloved Governor and the face of a new generation of leadership. So stop acting like a pussy and go out there and show them who's in charge!"

Connor shook his head, desperately wanting the nightmarish image to dissolve in the misty day. His grandfather might not have been around, but somehow a bully still bellowed in his ear. The small, slick tyrant screaming inside the car matched all his grandfather's ire in a body half the size. Stanley Grayson, known in the highest level political circles as the Kingmaker, had been Connor's campaign manager for less than two months. Two long, infuriating months filled with more fantasies of physical violence than Connor had ever had.

Keep the end in sight, man. He had to keep reminding himself that it was an honor that Stanley had agreed to work with him. His best friend's dad, Congressman Winston, aka Uncle Robert, had called in some big favors to make it happen. But they hadn't stopped butting heads. Stanley wanted to run things old school - and by old school, he meant wheeling, dealing, and dirty - while Connor wanted to do it better. He wanted to show all the people disillusioned by politics and their leaders that someone would have their back.

It wasn't working. Maybe he wasn't cut out for this after all.

The window slid halfway down. "Get your ass back in here!"

Connor paused before sauntering back to the car, taking his time to open the door and take a seat. He plastered a calm

3

expression on his face. "I was waiting for you to finish your phone call, Stanley. No need for all that yelling."

"You better get your head in the game, Barrett! I was on the phone with the morning show, arguing for you to get top billing. This is NOT the time to be checking out."

Connor exhaled, praying for patience. "I'm not checking out."

Stanley tightened his lips to a nearly invisible line. "Could have fooled me... Anyway. Tonight is extremely important. Most of the big guns will be here, deciding whether you're going to be their chosen horse in this race."

Connor flinched at being referred to as a horse. This guy was disgusting. "I understand that."

"Do you? Because you've turned it into a family party. This is not the time to socialize with your buddies. This is the time to make an impression on the power players with deep pockets. They are going to determine whether you even make it to the primaries, much less the main election."

No shit. It was exhausting having this conversation over and over. "That's clear. And that's why Ramona is here. She-"

"Your knocked-up sister? She's the problem, not the solution, Barrett. No one wants to see a woman flaunting her promiscuity around like that. As if the scandal with the Winston boy wasn't bad enough..."

Connor vaulted forward in his seat, fist clenched against his side. It had been years since he'd hit someone but it might not be much longer. "Don't you fucking dare talk about my sister that way! You and I both know she is the most talented fundraiser on this planet. I'm lucky she agreed to do anything for me, after the stunt you pulled on New Year's Eve. You," he pointed right in the man's face, "are not allowed within ten feet of her. Understood?"

The older man slid back, that self-satisfied smirk on his

face. Again. "Now, that's more like it. That's the kind of fire people are waiting to see in you. That's the stuff that's going to get you a seat in that very impressive building down the street."

And this was how it went. Stanley got to be as offensive as he wanted to be, then shrugged it off as part of the plan. Connor pulled off his glasses and rubbed his eyes, working to manage the rage that brought a throb around his temples. If this was the price he had to pay to get elected, he would have to pay it. There just didn't seem like another option.

THE CATERERS SCURRIED as Connor wound his way through the prep kitchen. Only a few stopped what they were doing to stare and whisper. He walked a little taller and put on his 'future Senator' face. Looking the part was half the game.

Stanley escorted him into the green room, where he'd wait until it was time for him to speak. He wasn't allowed out until that point, probably because Stanley didn't trust him to not say something wrong. *As if.* Connor Barrett had his faults but saying the wrong thing wasn't one of them.

He was grateful Stanley had to step out to deal with some emergency or another. A minute away from that man was good for his mental health. Congressman Winston—Uncle Robert—arrived a few minutes later. During all those hard years when his family was shredded - Mom fleeing to California, Dad lost in the bottle, Granddad on the war path - he'd depended more and more on his best friend's family. Lucas Winston was more like a brother than a friend and his dad, a longtime Congressman, had been the one to support Connor in his political journey. He'd done so much to make this evening happen, it was hard to express enough thanks.

"Uncle Robert. So glad to see you."

The man put his palm on Connor's face. "Lookin' good, kid. Are you excited?"

Excited? Terrified, more like it. "Yes, I am. We've got a full house and-"

"You know, I remember my first big rally, when I decided to leave my position in the State Senate and run for Congress. I don't think I stopped shaking for days. I get what a big deal this is. But your time has come. Virginia needs you. Our country needs you."

The two men hugged briefly before Robert pulled away. "Now, who do I have to fuck to get a drink around here?"

Two YOUNG WOMEN carried trays into the room minutes after Connor's call to the catering manager. He was surprised Stanley didn't breeze in after them, admonishing him about the food they'd requested.

"Never eat before a speech," he'd say. "It makes you look fat and lazy. You want to look hungry. That's what sells."

The women set up the table in the center of the room with a bottle of Scotch, several bottles of water, and an assortment of the appetizers he assumed were being served to the guests. He caught Robert enjoying the view, a bit too much. A pat on the back pulled Robert's attention from an admittedly fine derriere back to Connor.

"Did you get the draft of my speech?"

"Sure did. Looks good." A quick glance back over at the women. "I'd say it's better to err on the side of too little than too much. These folks won't be lingering over their decisions. And our speeches are just going to get in the way of them eating, drinking, and talking about themselves."

He was probably right. You didn't get to be a Congressman for so many decades if you didn't know what to do in these situations. "Okay, maybe I'll cut some from the middle."

Robert slapped him on the back. "Just be yourself, Connor. Have a conversation with the crowd. You're naturally charismatic. Use it. The women will be swooning, the men will remember when they were as young and handsome as you. It'll be fine. Just fine."

The two women snuck a look before disappearing out the door. He could have sworn the blonde actually winked at him.

Robert smirked. "It's good we got some nice looking waitresses, too. That always helps. Especially, if you're looking for some company tonight." He winked. "After the rally."

Not going to happen. By the time the VIP after-party was done, it was going to be late. Then he had his regular workout first thing in the morning and a day full of appointments. Although, it had been a long time since he'd had another outlet for all that energy of his. And it would probably be a while before he could go out and bang just anyone.

Young and single was not necessarily a kiss of death for a male Senator, but it rarely helped. He had to make sure he wasn't coming across as a player. Gotta promote those conservative values, as Stanley reminded him. Frequently.

He pulled out his phone and jotted down a note to talk to Lorena, his matchmaker, the next day. So far, all her offerings had been duds. Too boring. Too chatty. Too wild. Too power-hungry. Dating, when you were on a fast track to a serious political position, was much more complicated than finding someone to warm your bed.

He needed a woman who was smart, serious, and driven, but not too much of either. Someone who understood the life of a political wife and wanted all that came with it. A busty brunette would be great. He would have thought in this part of the world, the streets would be teeming with that type of woman. So far, no luck. Especially since Lorena kept insisting on sending him blondes, who were almost always an immediate *no*.

This woman, wherever she was, had to be White House ready.

CHAPTER 2

*J*enna fought her way through the crowd like a salmon swimming upstream. She had no interest in following everyone toward the stage, where an older man was droning on about government and the future and blah blah blah. With everyone's attention on Mr. Boring Pants, it was a perfect time to head toward the now empty bar.

The impressive collection of high-end bottles sparkled under a web of pinlights. Not bad. Could rival any of the fanciest bars she'd seen. Not that she liked fancy bars. Dark-and-dirty was more her speed. This being her very first political rally, she wasn't aware of the high caliber alcohol they would serve. Her favorite tequila, in fact.

She eyed the young bartender. Also not bad. Maybe she could rescue this ultra-dull evening after all.

"A shot of Patron platinum, please."

He nodded and reached toward the recognizable bottle. "Aren't you interested in hearing the candidate speak?"

"Not even a little bit."

"Then why are you here?" he asked with a smirk.

She preferred her bartenders hot and silent, and this one

was only fulfilling one of those desires. "He's a friend of the family, supposedly." *And a free trip across the country is better than working.* "They're all here to support him, so I had to come, too. But we don't even live in this state and can't vote for him. I don't see the point, honestly."

The crowd burst into applause as the generous shot slid down her grateful throat. The opening act must have finished and the main guy—the candidate—would be speaking next. Oh, yay. More political speeches about governing this tiny, inconsequential state.

The huddled bodies separated just enough for Jenna to see the tall, dark-haired man stride across the stage. Her eyes followed his every move as she became aware of three things.

1. He had terrible taste in clothes.

2. She remembered him from old family photos, running circles in their backyard wearing thick glasses and a bright red cape.

3. That swagger communicated something to her body that she would never have expected.

She turned away, slightly disturbed, but couldn't keep her eyes off him. That guy was not her type at all. Unless, of course, underneath that baggy blue suit and those nerdy glasses was a wild streak and a back full of tattoos. But the way he owned the stage and captured the crowd woke up several regions of her body.

She ended up listening, rapt, to his thankfully brief speech about his candidacy for Senate. People were excited. She guessed having a young, almost-hot Senator might not be so bad if you were forced to live there.

The applause continued long after he'd walked away from the podium and disappeared into the mass of people huddled around the stage. Unease kept her gaze fixed on the crowd. It's not that she wanted another opportunity to see him. Find out what he looked like up close. Nope. Not at all.

Jenna forced herself to turn toward the bar, which was considerably more crowded than when she'd first arrived. She considered the bartender, the tequila, and the possibilities for each, deciding after some time that neither would be a good idea. Which left her getting pushed about by the folks trying to get her coveted spot.

An older man barked an order at the bartender and Jenna shifted over a few feet to protect her ears from the abusive boom of his voice. Even more bodies filled the space. She'd expected at this point to be heading to the next event, with more dull speeches, fake smiles, and pot-bellied men. All these eager voters should've been off to their next Saturday night activity, lame as they might have been. Her plans would be fine as long as they included more high-quality booze.

A scan of the dense crowd did not reveal any of her family members. She'd need to find them at some point, if only to get the okay to ditch this scene and find something to do that wasn't utterly boring. She ran her palm across the top of her hair, assuring that not a single strand was out of place, and fiddled with her necklace. *Patience, Jenna.*

If departure was not in her near future, a run to the bathroom might be necessary. She spun around and bumped into the center of a broad chest. Bland blue filled her vision. It was him.

"Oh, sorry, I didn't know you were right behind me." Squeaky words tumbled out of her mouth.

A squint followed one of the goofiest smiles she'd ever seen. All loopy and happy, with no smolder whatsoever. "Jenna King, right? Wow, you look so much like your mom. And your Aunt Olivia. It's uncanny."

Right. Olivia Winston was her aunt and his best friend's

mom. Resident bitch of Virginia, far as Jenna could tell. Her fingers tapped the mass of hair currently contained in a low bun. The only similarity she had with those two women was the platinum blonde hair no one ever believed was real.

He put out his hand. "I'm Connor Barrett. Thanks so much for coming. Your family has been amazingly supportive."

"Hey." She returned his handshake. "Oh, and congratulations on the... running for office."

He laughed. "Thanks. What are you drinking?"

"Oh, you did well with the bar selection. Patron platinum. Yumm. Way to schmooze the voters."

He put up two fingers for the bartender who was standing at attention, and had finally figured out how to keep his mouth shut.

Two overfull shot glasses appeared on the bar.

He tipped his head toward her. "Cheers."

It had only been minutes since her last shot, but the new one went down oh, so smoothly. She licked a drop of tequila from her top lip and grinned.

He threw his down and instead of the flinch and gag she expected, he smiled right back at her. "Only the best for my supporters."

That look was so hard to decipher. And it was impossible to see his eyes behind those thick, dark frames. But there was definitely something she recognized in his face. "I think we met when we were kids. I don't really remember it, though."

"Me neither. But I remember your older brother."

Of course. Her superstar brother. "Yeah, Jackson's pretty memorable. I was really little and probably inconsequential."

"I can't imagine that ever being true, but I'm glad to meet you again."

Jenna shifted her weight from one foot to the other,

remembering about her interrupted trip to the bathroom. He wasn't speaking. Or moving out of her way.

"So, tell me something about yourself. What do you do?"

She looked around at the line forming behind him. Wow, what an orderly group of people, patiently waiting their turn to talk to the man of the day. "I'm a schoolteacher. Middle school history."

"Tell me about middle school history. I'm kind of a history buff myself."

The warm tingle of alcohol entering her bloodstream sent warmth to her cheeks. At least, she thought it was the alcohol. "You know, I really thought it was going to work. I thought, if I get them young enough, if I show them the lessons we've learned, over and over, then maybe they would think differently. Act differently. I was top of my class in school – sociology and political science double major. I know stuff that can help them make a difference in the world. Make better choices. Understand the patterns and cycles that are consistent and predictable."

Had he moved even closer to her? It felt like all she could see was blue.

A small smile tipped the corners of his mouth up. "I'm getting that it's not quite working out that way."

"Well, the first problem is that I'm working in an elite private school. I'm basically a servant to the tyrannical parents and their little despots-in-training. I have absolutely no power, no influence, no impact."

"That sounds pretty shitty."

The tequila was loosening her inhibitions and her lips. "Yeah. I really wanted to make a difference. Bring forth a new way of leading people, of being benevolent stewards of our communities, maybe of this country."

"Why not go into politics yourself?"

"It's not for me. I'm not interested in dealing with what a woman like me would have to put up with just to be heard. I think politics used to be the meeting ground for grand ideas and high ideals. Now it's the last stop for the greedy, power-hungry, and ignorant."

She didn't understand the shocked look on his face at first. Then it dawned on her that she was attending a political rally. *His* political rally.

Her hand flew up to cover her mouth. Too bad all that nonsense had already slipped out. "Holy shit! I'm so sorry."

He burst out laughing. "Jenna King, you are the most interesting person I've encountered in this whole room. No one talks like that anymore, which I think is part of the problem. We're not addressing the reality of the matter. We're just tap-dancing around all of it."

Relief returned in the form of a deep breath. She had to learn how to hold her tongue at some point. Maybe less tequila, too. "I meant no offense. Maybe you're the exception."

"I want to be."

Something about how he said that made her believe him. Wow. This guy knew something about wielding power.

He tipped his head toward her, those whisky-brown eyes finally coming into view. "I've got a proposition."

She flinched involuntarily.

All the humor left his expression. "No, not like that. Come work with me. I'm putting together my team and someone like you would make a great addition. I want the truth, as blunt and inappropriate as it may be. I haven't yet met someone I trusted to give it to me."

Well, that was exciting. "I don't live here, Connor. I live in California."

"Doesn't matter. Come here for the next ten months,

assuming I make it through the primaries. Then you can go back to your bratty students in California."

He touched her arm, which would normally have sent off alarms, but there was nothing sexual or predatory about it. Interesting.

"I have to tell you, Connor, that's one of the most intriguing propositions I've gotten in a long time." Truth. In fact, the last request a man had made of her was *Get the fuck out.*

"Then it's a yes?"

"You seem like a good guy. I know my family thinks so. But I can't leave my life, move across the country, and learn everything about political campaigns. Thanks, but no."

Besides politics is boring.

Someone tapped Connor on the shoulder. Before turning to acknowledge Mrs. Tappy Hands, he looked Jenna in the eye. Yeah, those big brown eyes were something.

"Thanks for chatting with me, Jenna. I look forward to seeing you at the party."

She blinked as if recovering from a shock while Connor turned to address the beaming couple behind him. "Hello. I appreciate your support."

JENNA SLIPPED past them and made her way toward the bathroom, running into her best friend and soon to be sister-in-law on the way.

"Jenna! Where've you been? We thought maybe you snuck out and headed out to a biker bar." Camille's typical composure had left the building.

"I wish. No, I was chatting up the candidate, if you must know."

"Really? I am actually surprised. But he was so inspiring. I almost wish I lived here, because he'd definitely have my vote." Camille stared up, all dreamy eyes.

Geez. Jenna knew it wasn't the hots. Camille had had it bad for Jenna's brother Jackson forever. And they'd just gotten engaged. So, that look on her face was, like, inspiration, or something. Weird. "Hmmm. So, what's next?"

"We're going back to the house. For a VIP party."

Oh, that party.

"You'll finally get to see the mansion. Not sure how much of it will be off limits because of the construction, but hopefully you'll get a sense of it."

Camille had been collaborating with Connor's sister, Ramona, for several months on a project to convert their grandfather's estate into a children's center. Jenna knew Ramona too, but not as well. Cool chick. But their family was straight out of a TV drama about the old South. The Barretts were some kind of old school political dynasty. Hopefully, more stately mansion than plantation. Either way, the supposed party sounded like a definite snooze-fest.

Jenna pretended to yawn. "Yeah. Soooo exciting."

Her best friend jabbed her in the ribs. "Can you stop being such a pain? I'm sure it won't last long, then you can make your way to the seediest, smelliest bar, and go find some burly, leather-clad dude to grind up on."

Jenna threaded her arm through Camille's and pulled her toward the bathroom. "Now, you're talking."

CHAPTER 3

"Thank goodness," Connor said, under his breath as he entered the empty green room, Stanley nowhere to be found. A small amount of tension released on an exhale. It was always nice, after the wild rush of a speech and a crowd, to have some time to regroup. Taking the energy back down helped him maintain an even keel.

The evening so far had gone even better than expected. He'd decided to wing part of his speech, make it more spontaneous, which was always a risk. He wasn't a wing-it kind of guy. Preparation was everything, especially in high stakes situations. Maybe Uncle Robert had been right. Taking it a bit more casually seemed to get a great response.

That conversation with Jenna King at the bar was going to have him smiling for some time. She basically called him a criminal to his face, and it was one of the most amusing things he'd ever experienced. She was a kick. That mouth on that face was a deadly combination.

His body surged with energy. The whole plan to calm down had been foiled thinking about the tall blonde. He stared down at his watch, hoping it would magically be an hour earlier than it actually was. He needed more time to burn off his nervous energy and excitement. A lung-crushing run would have done the trick, but there was no way he'd be allowed to disappear for that long. Stanley would be bursting through the door any second and they had to get to the mansion.

The fast clip of footsteps meant Stanley was close. The door swung open. "All right, Barrett. Time to go."

Connor took one more deep breath before heading out the service entrance to the waiting car.

THEY PULLED into the circular driveway of the mansion, lined with cars, with a handful of young people working as valets. Ramona had done an amazing job with this whole night. Professional to a T.

It had been generous of his sister to offer the use of their grandfather's mansion, which now belonged to her and had become her pet project. It was one of the most famous homes in Virginia - on the historic registry - and it was a bold move for her to make.

She'd had to stop construction and get huge sections of the house blocked off. He thought it was too much, but she insisted. The fact that his grandfather was a legend in the state was going to bring in important, powerful supporters. That's probably the only thing Ramona and Stanley, the most chauvinistic person Connor had ever met, agreed on.

Unlike the tiny bully, his sister was a gladiator. Upended her life to move back to Virginia, rekindle a relationship with Lucas, their childhood buddy, and build a state-of-the art children's center. The whole pregnancy thing hadn't been in her plans, but he had no doubt she'd land on her feet. She always did.

"You did a nice job today, Barrett. That speech was right on."

Connor startled, pulled out of his thoughts and floored that something complimentary had just come out of Stanley's mouth.

"Uh... thanks. Uncle Robert gave me some pointers."

"See? Those are the kind of guys you want to emulate. No need to blaze a new trail or any of that nonsense. Men like Congressman Robert Winston knew what they had to do to get elected. And to *keep* getting elected. You model yourself after him and you'll have no trouble."

Connor remembered the leering look Robert had given those waitresses. The same look that his own uncles, all in politics, typically had on their smug faces. He had no interest in modeling that particular behavior. "Got it."

"So, you're going to be on your own tonight. Can you handle it?"

Connor bit his tongue against yet another slight. As if he was a child. "Of course. It's close friends and family, and I'm hoping to keep it casual. Comfortable."

"This isn't social hour. And it isn't just friends and family. These are some of your most powerful potential allies. Your job is to secure their commitment and loyalty."

My job is to ply them with food and drink, impress them with the governor's mansion, then stick my hand out for money. "I understand."

"Good. See you at the team meeting tomorrow morning." Stanley exited the car, leaving Connor with a sense of relief. He leaned back in his seat and closed his eyes. The quiet couldn't have been more welcome.

"Excuse me, Mr. Barrett?"

His driver's voice pulled him from of an oddly persistent image of a tall blonde. Alex had been their family's driver for years and one of Connor's favorite people. "Yes, Alex."

"Mr. Grayson had informed me to drop you off at the side entrance. Would you like to sit here for a minute before we go? Then the car won't be seen..."

"Brilliant, as always." One day, Connor was going to insist that they go out for a meal together. Or a drink. Although he supposed insisting did not help their power balance. Alex was only ever professional, even when Connor attempted to extend a hand of friendship. "If I haven't told you recently, Alex, I'm grateful for all you've done for me and my family. You could have easily walked away from the crazy Barretts after my grandfather passed, but you chose to stay. It means a lot to me."

"Thank you, sir." Their brown eyes met in the rearview mirror. "It's exciting for me, too. I've known you since before you could walk. And now look at you."

Connor caught the broad smile that filled Alex's bronzed face, emphasizing the deep lines around his eyes and cheeks.

"You're going to do great things, Mr. Barrett. I'm not a gambling man, but I would put money on that."

Connor clasped Alex's shoulder. "I appreciate that, Alex. But let's just see if I don't get eliminated in the primaries."

Connor leaned back in his seat once again. A familiar image popped up behind his eyes. He was running, always in those old-fashioned outfits like the one Roger Bannister wore when he broke the four-minute mile. There he was, in the middle of the pack, pushing his way through, but getting blocked every few feet. Then an opening materialized and although his body was exhausted, he mustered one last surge of energy and pushed through. When he got to the finish line, he was wearing a bright red cape. The crowd went wild.

"It's going to be fine, sir. You will discover you have much more within you than you believe." Connor let Alex's words penetrate him. In the collection of wise voices he was lucky enough to have in his life, Alex's was near the top.

CONNOR MADE his way from the servant's entrance, winding his way up the back stairs to the library. Guests were being held in the ballroom until he descended the main staircase for his grand entrance. The ridiculous choreography felt a little too *Gone With the Wind* for his liking, but Stanley had insisted. Even though the little man wasn't there, Connor was sure that room was full of his spies ready to report back any deviation from the plan.

He paused in the center of the grand room and inhaled, taking in the smell of leather and old books. This had always been his favorite room in the house. He and his sister had spent hours in there as kids, awed by their grandfather's towering walls full of books. And hiding from him, too. As long as they were in the library, it was assumed they would be studying and learning. Keeping out of trouble. Which meant they were mostly left to themselves and out from under his oppressive thumb.

Connor glanced at the worn, brown leather chair where they both used to sit, holding the books they tried to read. His legs would dangle off the edge while Ramona would curl herself into a little ball. They helped each other with words they didn't understand. Although Ramona was younger, that girl was smart. Too smart. And she knew it.

He smiled at the memory, but had no interest in sitting down. If he could get away with a quick set of pushups, maybe even some jumping jacks, he would have. But the floors would creak, and he'd get all sweaty, and... Just not a good idea.

He took a long step and bent his knees. The small lunge only reinforced how much his body was aching for a workout. He switched legs. In the vice-filled world he lived in, his workout addiction could hardly be judged. Anyway, it had turned him from a ninety-pound weakling to a man. Maybe not compared to his crazy buff best friend Lucas, but the ladies seemed to like his lean frame well enough.

He grunted. Women. Before he spiraled down the dark hole of the woman missing from his life, Ramona and Lucas walked into the room.

"There you are!" His sister raised her arms in the air.

He curled his lip. "What?"

"We were waiting for you in the prep kitchen. Lucas had the idea to look up here."

He'd forgotten. The plan was to meet them downstairs before coming up. Oops. "Oh, yeah, sorry. I forgot. So much going on..."

She straightened his tie. "Okay. We found you, anyway."

It was crazy that not even a week ago, they had been in the biggest fight of their lives. Ramona had an aversion to politics. He couldn't blame her, based on their childhood, but he needed her support anyway. Thankfully, he'd pulled his head out of his ass, and she'd done the same. There's no way he could do this without her. Their mother would be back to the jungle any day now, and Ramona was the only family he had. Or could rely on.

He wrapped his arms around her. "Love you, Mo."

She squeezed back. "Love you, Con."

Lucas huddled in. "Love you, guys!"

Even after going over the schedule for the night, confirming the timing for the tours and private meetings, he still had twenty minutes before he could head down to the party. Marching in place, he pulled out his phone and checked social media. Someone kept trying to create a flurry around #ConManforSenate. Thankfully, it hadn't been catching on, but he still checked. Every day.

He could hear Ramona and Lucas talking while he scrolled his media feeds. He looked up just as Lucas planted a dramatic kiss on his sister, then immediately turned away. It's not that he wasn't happy for them. He really was. The three of them had been inseparable as kids, but he always knew that his sister and his best friend had a little something more than he had with either of them. He was cool with it.

It was a miracle they'd made their way back to each other, after all those years apart, too. And frankly, he couldn't imagine anyone better suited than his difficult sister and his demanding best friend. They were a fairytale. If he believed in such things.

He snuck a look. Still making out. A breath, as loud as he could muster, huffed out of him. It's just that Ramona had been stridently single, and Lucas hadn't even been trying to find love. They tripped into the relationship of a lifetime. Even Jackson, Lucas' cousin and the most renowned playboy on two coasts, was about to get married to Camille. All around him, people were settling into blissful couple-hood, and he was dangling out there like a lost thread. Where was the love of his life?

They were still embracing when he cleared his throat. "Are you guys done yet? I've got an election to win."

It felt like hours before they broke contact.

His sister gave him that look. The one she shared with their mother. Equal parts love, impatience, and disdain. "What can we do for you, Con?"

"Isn't it time yet?" He was acting like a cranky kid. *Grow up, man.*

Ramona checked her watch. "Let me do this. I'll go downstairs and confirm everyone's properly sequestered. We don't want some stray interrupting your grand entrance. I'll give you a thumbs-up text when we're good to go. Okay?"

He swallowed his embarrassment at being such a baby. "Yeah. Sounds great. Thanks."

She gave Lucas a quick kiss before disappearing down the hallway.

"Hey, Con. You doing all right?" Lucas' voice was full of concern.

"Yeah, just too much energy."

Lucas nodded. He, of anyone, knew what it was like when Connor didn't get a chance to work out all his tension. "You're going to be down there, with your adoring fans, any minute now. Then all that energy is going to wow them. Just a few more minutes."

"I know, man. I just hate waiting."

Lucas clasped his shoulder.

Connor needed to change the subject. "So, tell me about your cousin, Jenna."

CHAPTER 4

*J*enna looked from face to face of the small group assembled around her, trying to decipher their expressions. Perhaps this audience hadn't been the most appropriate for her extended rant about the failings of government and ignorance about the cycles of history. She just couldn't help herself.

They'd all been hoarded into a ballroom and left to wait for the guest of honor, who had taken his damn time. With the tequila mostly worn off, all the political masturbation was more than she could stomach quietly. Someone had to say something.

She'd had to listen to what felt like hours of bullshit and posturing. This should have been the perfect crowd to foster a meaty discussion, but there was nothing but twisted truth being flung about. Maybe she'd gotten confused by the initial earnestness of the people around her. The contrast with her normal experiences was palpable.

Instead of disdain and disrespect, whispered calls of Barbie, and conversations about her ass, they looked in her eyes, listened, and nodded with serious expressions. Made her think she was being heard and not just ogled. But all she got in response to her impassioned argument was a bunch of raised eyebrows and pursed lips.

Those expressions looked a lot like horror. Maybe her tone had been wrong. She sure as hell knew her arguments weren't faulty. Perhaps this gentile crowd wasn't ready for so much *truth*.

She smiled, hoping to diffuse the tension. If she stood silently, maybe they'd forget all about what she'd just said.

Ramona was the first to speak. "I'm just going to go ahead and say it."

Jenna flinched, preparing herself to be admonished. She and Ramona had gotten friendly, but she might have crossed the line. Ramona could well tell her off.

"We need you. That was one of the most perceptive and eloquent accounts of the biggest political mess of my lifetime. We need you, Jenna. Please come work with my brother. He's got a huge political fight, trying to unseat an incumbent who's failing but popular. He needs this type of insight."

Before Jenna could wrap her head around what had just come out of Ramona's mouth, a deeper voice sounded from behind her.

"Way ahead of you, sis," Connor added.

Jenna hadn't realized he'd been there, listening. Yikes. "I..."

He stepped beside her. "I've already offered her a position on the team. She's *exactly* who we need."

A collective nod passed through the crowd, who then muttered their agreement and splintered into smaller discussions. Everyone began talking about her as if she wasn't actually standing there with Connor's form looming above her and Ramona's eyes burrowing in.

Why was Ramona adding to the insanity? She knew

Jenna couldn't just up and move to Virginia to work on her brother's senatorial campaign. It was completely unrealistic.

She scanned the crowd, busy with their now private discussions, choosing to address Ramona and Connor directly. "That's very nice of you to say. I'm flattered." She decided against a more specific rebuttal. It was all preposterous.

Camille wove into the dissolving circle. Thank goodness.

Jenna reached for her friend's hand. "Cammy, let's go get something to eat." Although her voice was all sweet on the outside, it was communicating one thing: *I'm done with this scene, let's split.*

"Good idea, Jen," Camille responded.

The two women walked over to the extravagant buffet set up alongside one wall of the ballroom. With the intricate inlaid flooring, enormous portraits, and chandeliers the size of her entire apartment, it looked like it could have been pulled directly out of a brochure from the twenties. Or some movie about the old south. This was the house Jenna had been hearing about for months. Where her best friend had been spending all her time, instead of at home with Jenna.

She lingered next to a steaming tray of greens. This was definitely not California cuisine. Whatever they did to vegetables down here made her feel like her arteries were hardening with each bite. Each mind-blowingly delicious bite. "They're hitting it pretty hard with the *come work on our campaign* speech."

"Because it's a brilliant idea. I don't know why you're being so dismissive."

Jenna spun to glare at her best friend. "Are you crazy?"

"I don't know if it's because you doubt how much you know, or if you're afraid of upending your life and taking such a big risk, but I think both of those issues are bullshit. This would solve all your problems. Get out of that job that's sucking your soul dry, get out from under your parents' control, and get a change of scenery. You and I both know that things haven't been going that great, Jen."

That statement was just the amount of truthful to really hurt. "I can't believe you're considering this seriously. It's absurd."

"Listen, I'm here all the time because Ramona and I are working on the kids' center. And if I'm here, then Jackson will be here too."

As if on cue, her brother Jackson arrived and gave his fiancée a kiss on the cheek.

Camille continued. "Your two favorite people will be here to support you. I adore Ramona, and Connor is amazing. And your cousin Lucas is here. I love this idea."

"Are you talking about Jenna moving here to help with the campaign? I love it too. It couldn't be more perfect. Solves all your problems."

Jenna rolled her eyes. "The two of you are starting to sound like the same person. It's sickening."

Jackson shrugged. "Regardless, the idea is worth considering."

This was going to take her appetite away. "I don't know anything about politics."

Her brother shrugged. "But you know about history, and about people, and about achieving a desired outcome. All your skills could be put to work."

Her big-brained, celebrity psychologist brother was about to be wearing her full plate of food. "You sound ridiculous, Jackson."

He gave her his *I know better than you* face. "Do I?"

Camille stepped between them. "Jen, I think it's worth considering. You were all gung-ho about joining the Peace Corps after college. Maybe think of this as your political

Peace Corps. The election is less than one year away, during which you could irreversibly change your life."

"Hmfff." That was the problem. Her life wasn't great. More like dull and frustrating, truth be told. But it was hers. She wasn't into all this bold move nonsense, like her father. And her brother. And her best friend. That's why she bailed on the Peace Corps. Too scary. Too many unknowns. She just wasn't up for grand adventures.

After filling her belly beyond full, Jenna retreated to a quiet spot, out of the way of the pop-up conversations she didn't want to have. She had no interest in any more of that *working on the campaign* foolishness. She'd said quite enough for one day.

Camille had gone off, showing people around the mansion with Ramona, and her brother was hobnobbing with the bigwigs. Or maybe they were hobnobbing with him. She had no idea where her parents were, maybe somewhere talking weddings with her aunt and uncle. Both Jackson and their cousin Lucas were getting married soon. As painful as the political discussions had been, talking about weddings might have been worse.

She welcomed the moment of quiet. From her vantage point, sitting in the corner, she could do what she loved most: watching people. And from her perch, she catalogued some interesting things about the party-goers:

1. There was no shortage of money or power, which she knew something about. Having a legendary father, a celebrity brother, and a mother who hadn't completely ditched her roots in the aristocratic gentry, kept power front and center in Jenna's life.

2. Everything felt much more conservative—the way

people dressed, spoke, and comported themselves. Thank goodness she'd heeded Camille's lead and went with the understated dress and hair tucked away. Her all black outfit of leggings, peek-a-boo blouse and chunky boots had gotten tossed to the side.

3. The energy was completely different than at home, too. People showed their excitement instead of trying so hard to be cool. Folks were fired up about Connor, and without knowing why, she started to feel it, too.

Nothing this exciting happened in her life, other than the occasional bar fight at some of her seedier haunts. Even that was getting boring. Maybe she'd ask Jackson what lit this place up. He must have psychoanalyzed everyone in the room by this point and would give her a full report to soothe all her curiosity.

A loud laugh erupted from a bunch of round-bellied men huddled around the bar. Cut crystal glasses with brown liquor filled most of the hands. Although she didn't regret cooling it on the tequila, and definitely didn't want to get mixed up in that bar crowd, a drink was sounding more and more appealing.

"Is it Jennifer? Or just Jenna?"

She jumped. A slow glance behind her revealed the man of the day. Gosh, he was sneaky. And light-footed. "Actually, it's Jenevieve. The French way."

The lights reflected off his glasses. "Wow. Quite a name."

Not the first time she'd heard that. "My mom is obsessed with all things French. Not sure how a farm girl from Virginia fell in love with France, but that's the story."

"Yeah, I remember that about Aunt Elena."

Jenna had to do a quick calculation about her relationship to Connor. No, they weren't cousins, but that good ole Southern hospitality had given her mother the title of Aunt.

Then she remembered that Connor was best friends with her cousin Lucas. She might need a chart to keep up with all of that.

His stare made the next few seconds of silence very uncomfortable. Too bad she couldn't think of a damn thing to say or a reason why she felt so awkward around him.

"I'm guessing France felt like everything Aunt Elena's life here wasn't: sophisticated, glamorous, elegant."

Another man who was too smart for his own good. Fantastic. "I think you might be right."

A shoulder quirked up. "That happens once in a while." He stepped closer to where she sat. "I know I'm right that you'd make a great addition to the team."

She swallowed. This was tiresome, but she didn't want to be rude. "I really appreciate all the nice things you're saying. I do. But what I know is the theory of politics. I don't have a clue about the reality of politics. Except that it's got to be significantly different, considering how everyone behaves. I don't think my knowledge, and my ideas, would be worth anything."

He paused, staring toward the large portrait of what must have been his grandfather. "I have a good sense about people. It's come in handy throughout my life. So, although you claim it's not something you know how to do, what I see is the possibility of a new way."

Damn! Eloquent, too. Sure, it sounded great when he put it that way. But realistically, there was no way she was moving across the country to work with someone she hardly knew doing something she had no clue about.

No way.

CHAPTER 5

*T*he party lasted much longer than Connor expected. It consistently surprised him how interested people were in him. He thought even Stanley would have approved at the amount of support he'd received, verbal and financial. Ramona would have the actual numbers, but from what he overheard, it was big.

No matter how many back slaps, Senate jokes, and big dollar promises he'd received, the real star had been Jenna. She wasn't even trying to get attention, mostly hiding in a corner, but he couldn't stop finding her, wherever she was. It was almost as if Madonna had shown up to his party. He wished he could understand why he felt pulled to her, like a set of magnets.

Other than having to occasionally duck into one of the house's many nooks to discretely adjust himself, he'd successfully played off how watching Jenna King made his dick dance. If it hadn't been so fun, watching her school all his guests, it might have been embarrassing. Whatever. What guy wouldn't be hot over a woman who looked like a movie star, even if she wasn't remotely his type?

The issue, he had to admit, was that it was more than just her looks. She communicated like someone who knew what they were talking about. No snake oil, inflation, or double-speak, which despite his life in politics, still made him cringe. She was logical and passionate at the same time. And then her laugh would reach across the room and grab him as she transformed from stern teacher to sex goddess.

His eyes had followed her as she crossed the room, arm-in-arm with Camille. He could imagine the two of them sauntering into a bar and all the other women shuffling out, defeated. Something about her reminded him of a wild cat. Streamlined, precise, but simmering with a power and energy that felt like it could devour him. Like a tiger. He wanted-

No! Stop thinking that kind of shit, Connor. Get your head in the game.

"Don't you agree?"

His eyes refocused on the eager face of the woman across from him. He had no idea what she'd been saying. "Yes, of course."

She smiled and batted her eyelashes. Uh oh. He hoped he hadn't just agreed to a date or something. "Great. I'm glad we're on the same page. It's important that the candidate I back feel strongly about this."

He touched her shoulder and squeezed the perfect non-sexual amount. "I'm glad to hear that, Miranda. Your support means everything."

She winked. "Well, you have it, Connor."

He didn't like that look on her face at all. It had become recognizable over the years, especially from the large numbers of neglected political wives. In addition to the obvious benefits of gender parity in the political system, it would help decrease the number of women discarded by their power-hungry husbands.

He bowed his head and excused himself. A rare moment, with no one waiting for his attention, presented itself so he snuck out to the kitchen. He was starving. It seemed like every time he was about to eat something, someone wanted to have a conversation. His sister was leaning against the large slab of marble in the middle of the kitchen, writing in a notebook, when he walked in.

"Hey, Mo."

She looked up, startled. "Hey. What are you doing here?"

"I need to throw some food down my throat before I bite someone's head off."

She nodded. His sister was familiar with the problem when Connor didn't have enough to eat. *Hangry* didn't begin to describe it. She opened up the industrial-sized fridge. "I can heat you up some of the chicken piccata the caterers made. With extra veggies."

A slow smile filled his face. Even though they'd lived on opposite sides of the country for all of their adulthood, and had nearly opposite personalities, he hardly loved anyone more than his little sister. She'd taken on the role of mother early on, and hadn't let it go. And now, she was going to be a mother. Wild.

"Hello... Earth to Connor." She waved her hand at him.

Her face. Beautiful, like their mom's. "Yeah, that sounds great. Thanks, sis."

CONNOR ENDED the evening in the cigar room with Jackson King, the man Connor had been watching nearly his whole life. Therapist to the stars and a celebrity in his own right, he made Connor's accomplishments look like a child's gold ribbon. In addition to the fact that Jackson looked every bit the part of superstar and playboy. Or former playboy, now that he was about to get married.

Although Jackson was Lucas' cousin, they'd all grown up together like family. All nearly the same age, but not so much else in common. Almost no one was a better conversationalist, and occasional mind-bender, than Jackson. Connor could learn a lot from him. If he could stop himself from asking about his sister Jenna, instead.

Jackson rolled his cigar between his thumb and pointer finger. "I think it's so cool how the Universe keeps bringing us together. Your sister and my fiancée are working together, Ramona and Lucas are an item, I'm doing some mediation work with Uncle Robert's committee... Who would have thought we'd go from those crazy touch football games to this?"

Connor nodded. He was right. Although they'd never lost touch, they certainly hadn't had this much overlap in years. Decades, even. "I think it's great. You know, we're all getting older, starting our lives and our families... It's good to stay connected to family. I know the short time I was in California, your parents were great to me."

"So, tell me, Con. What can I do to help you with this campaign? My highest level contacts aren't DC-based, unfortunately, but I've got a great network of PR people, stylists, speech writers, media, anything else you need. And I'm glad to introduce you to any of the big money folks I know. I want to help."

Connor drew on his cigar. He'd regret it in the morning, but it was a rare treat. "Thanks so much, Jackson. I really appreciate it. Right now, Stanley's taking care of most of that. He and I have some... stylistic differences, so I'd love to bring some like-minded folks onto the team, too."

Jackson finished the thought before Connor could. "Like Jenna."

A sip of cognac created the perfect burn in his throat. "Yeah. I mean, I wouldn't call her like-minded, but I love her ideas. That's the kind of straight-shooting I need. I'm afraid Stanley will just surround us with yes-men."

Jackson swirled his cognac, the large glass nestled in his palm. "That rarely does anybody any good."

"But I know it's too much to ask. Crazy, actually. She's not interested. So, I'll keep scouting." Disappointing as that felt.

Jackson took a sip and perched forward. "The thing about my sister is..." He paused as if considering his words. "You see, she was really babied by my parents. My father, especially. Only girl, you know. And although she's one of the smartest, most capable, natural leaders I've ever known, she's never seen that in herself."

This was interesting. "Hmmmm..."

"I don't think anyone would argue that I'm an ambitious person. So are my brothers. But Jenna..."

Connor had no idea where this was going.

Jackson blew out a breath. "Jenna might be the most competitive and ambitious person I've ever known."

Connor's face broke out in surprise. "Really?"

"It's just that being born a woman who looks like she does, things get confusing. I know my parents didn't encourage that part of her development, either. So she got stuck being the smart, beautiful girl who didn't threaten anyone. And then the smart, beautiful woman who got used to things being easier than they should be."

This was all fascinating, if not highly uncomfortable. He'd never been given a stranger's psychological profile.

"She graduated cum laude from Princeton, then got this

job as a middle school teacher. Hell, I'm not against teaching, but I think that she didn't believe there was anything more for her. And it turns out she hates it. It doesn't suit her at all. So, she's doing everybody a disservice - herself and those kids."

Connor had an image of her disciplining a room full of unruly kids. Dressed like an old-time schoolteacher, ruler in hand. Damn if it didn't make his dick twitch. Again.

Jackson kept going. "Jenna puts on this bold, rebellious persona - she's always pushing against limits - but underneath, she's scared. Doesn't see herself as powerful. All her subversive tendencies are an attempt to access that power, but they're misdirected."

Connor's head was spinning and he knew it wasn't the cognac.

Jackson pointed his finger. "I think her coming here to work with you is a brilliant idea. Just what she needs. And the synergy between the two of you is remarkable."

Connor jerked with the cigar inches from his face. "The synergy?"

Jackson laughed. "Oh, sorry. I'm always analyzing the way people interact. Professional hazard, I suppose. And the two of you have this yin-yang thing going. But that's just on the surface. I think your true ethics and beliefs are totally in line. That's what makes a relationship work."

Connor stayed frozen. He couldn't tell if Jackson was talking about a *relationship* or working together.

"You look confused. What I mean is that there's a high probability of you being able to work together quite successfully. My only concern would be for your current campaign manager. She knows how to bring authority figures to their knees."

Connor wanted to feel relieved, maybe even humored,

but all that came forward was frustration at not being able to get what he wanted. "Right. But there's still the reality that she doesn't want to work with me. It's not like I can force her."

Jackson leaned back in the plush chair and smiled. "I think she would love this work. Let me see what I can do."

CHAPTER 6

Four months later

*J*enna dragged a chair to the center of the tent and stood on it, steady even on her heels. The tent was bustling with activity and she needed to be heard over the din. "Okay, everyone, it's almost showtime!"

The noise level dropped as if someone had flipped a switch. All eyes and ears tuned to her.

"You've done an extraordinary job making today happen, and I want you to know how much you're appreciated." She wiped her forehead, catching a drop of sweat before it broke free and rolled down the side of her face. All those bodies crammed into this tent on a blazing hot day reminded her of a sweat lodge.

"I know it's hot. I know you're all tired. But let's keep our eyes on the prize. We've come this far. Let's bring it home, one day at a time."

Remarkably, they took their exhausted bodies and whooped and hollered their agreement. Jenna looked down on the sea of faces – young, old, men, women, every race, who, like her, had put their lives on hold to elect a man who represented the possibility for a better world.

Her assistant, Luisa, tapped her arm. How did that woman stay so cool looking, as if it wasn't a million degrees outside? Her dark brown skin and long braids pulled into a swirl of a bun never showed any sign that they had been working nonstop for weeks. Or that it was like a steam room in that tent. "Jenna, CNN's still waiting for a statement."

"Right." A bead of sweat slid down her back. "Tell them I'll be with them in exactly four minutes."

Luisa pivoted and took several long strides toward the exit. She could well have been strutting down a red carpet. Jenna would have to take some walking lessons from hern.

"Thank you!" Jenna shouted across the room. Although it was meant for Luisa, it could have easily applied to anyone else there.

She stepped down off the chair to address the small group waiting patiently for their turn to have their questions addressed. Jenna had trained them well in speaking concisely and taking notes so information wouldn't have to be repeated —another skill she'd perfected with her history students. One by one, she answered every inquiry and sent them on their way to the next task. It often felt as if she was back in the classroom, except the belligerent teenagers were now smart, capable humans passionate about their assignments and eager to please.

She checked her phone as she headed toward the back of the tent. Five minutes to showtime. Just enough time to confirm Connor was wired correctly. The last AV guy had really screwed it up, so it had become one of Jenna's personal tasks. She spotted his dark hair, towering over everyone else in that room.

He greeted her approach with a broad smile. "How's my favorite campaign manager?"

Her smile flipped to a frown in lightning speed.

"What?" He looked down with a scowl. "What's wrong?"

She curled her lip and huffed. "Take off your shirt."

The look changed from confused to incredulous. "But I love this sh-"

"Dammit, Connor, take off your shirt. Now."

"But-"

She grabbed handfuls of the fabric around his abdomen and pulled the end of the dress shirt out of his pants, then reached up and began unbuttoning.

He batted her hands away. "Okay, okay, you don't like the shirt. I get it."

One hand flew to her headset. "Pit stains. Nobody's going to vote for a guy with pit stains."

He reached the last button and stopped. "But it's ninety degrees out there."

"Doesn't matter." She pressed a button on her phone. "Alex, please bring the spares, as quickly as possible."

The shirt came off, leaving him in a white undershirt.

She looked him in the eye. "Everything."

It was his turn to huff.

As usual, Connor was being a pain. "That's sweaty, too. Must you make everything more difficult?"

At this point, much of the staff had been alerted that Connor Barrett was going to be shirtless. All the frenzy and rushing slowed to a near standstill. No one wanted to miss the sight of his magnificent bare chest. A few of the younger women might have even gasped. Jenna kept her gaze up and away from the heat-inducing sight.

Jenna recognized the weightier thump of Alex's footsteps

and reached behind her for the delivery of the new shirts. "Thank you, Alex. You're the best."

"My pleasure, Ms. King," the deep voice sounded from behind her.

She handed Connor a fresh t-shirt, then helped him on with the crisp white dress shirt. Pit stains resolved. She straightened his collar as he tucked in the shirt.

"I can dress myself, you know."

She raised one eyebrow.

"Although, you clearly do it better than I do."

She surveyed her work while he buttoned his cuffs. Perfect. "Okay, now go out there and remind them one more time how much they love you."

She didn't wait for his answer before bolting for the other side of the tent. She pressed her headset again. "Luisa, I'm headed out the front. Don't want to miss him walking on stage. Will do CNN from there."

She stepped out of the tent, surprised it was only slightly less stifling outside than inside, and searched for a shady spot. There was only one option, near a dogwood tree, where she'd have a full view of the stage. Watching Connor do his thing was one of the highlights of her job.

Connor was pretty far behind in the race, but because of his family's reputation, still received plenty of media attention. Jenna had gotten a lightning fast education in handling media and she hardly broke a sweat, no matter how important the news outlet or interviewer.

She clicked over to the waiting call. "Hello, this is Jenna King."

Although it might have been a better idea to be somewhere quieter, she wouldn't miss Connor walking out to the waiting crowd. With her attention on the stage, she fielded the questions with ease. The reporter's nondescript voice and simple questions faded into the background as Jenna's body took in Connor's entrance.

All the swagger she'd spotted at the event so many months before had only intensified. With every speech, every rally, every interview, his confidence had grown. He'd learned a lot about public speaking from Stanley, but it was the moments when he relaxed and followed his own instincts that he really shined on stage or camera. She just needed to convince him to let go of all of his precious rules and be himself. Stanley had done a number on him, claiming he had to become a totally different person. She shook her head, another drop of sweat sliding down the back of her neck.

What an asshole that guy had been. Pretty much terrorized all the men and harassed all the women. The day of the screaming match that ended with Stanley storming out, all the remaining staff had cried together with happiness. Too bad the team had been decimated at that point. But they trusted her to rebuild it. *He* trusted her.

While the crowd applauded, Connor paced a few steps toward her and smiled. No matter how things turned out with this campaign, she knew that something miraculous had happened in her life. Far away from her family and her simple life, she discovered that she was a natural leader. She could take charge, and not just of demonic teenagers. Despite being short-staffed, the current team kicked ass. She couldn't have asked for a better group of workers and volunteers. Or a better boss.

Every day, he became more impressive. What he stood for, how he comported himself in the world. And of course, the long, lean, muscular frame. And those eyes...

Stop it, Jenna. Drooling over her boss was never a good idea, and worse yet in this high stakes situation. Best case, they'd be working together for another five months and she needed to keep her cool. Getting him into the Senate was more important than whatever was happening between her legs. She shifted her weight. A lot was happening.

He did one of his signature moves, patting his palm on his heart, while promising them his devout service. A glance out into the crowd confirmed the mass of mesmerized women. At least she wasn't the only one.

A welcome breeze kept the inferno at bay. If she had been at home in San Francisco, she'd still be wearing sweaters and boots. It was inhuman how hot and muggy Virginia was. And it wasn't even summer yet.

A new joke brought a round of laughter through the crowd. He was killing it. She'd had doubts about the new speechwriter - he seemed a bit too hip and cool for the conservative campaign - but the new material was good. The infusion of humor worked for Connor. Made him seem like less of a stiff. She'd make sure to let Gabe know he'd done well when she saw him later at the team meeting.

It was funny how Gabe and Connor were stark opposites, but apparently had been friends since attending Georgetown together. Gabe was all smooth and suave, always meticulously dressed, and had the hots for her from the moment he joined the team. Under other circumstances, he might have made a nice diversion - especially to take her mind off of her inappropriate infatuation - but it was too close. And something told her that Connor wouldn't be pleased at all if she started doing his gorgeous friend. She knew Connor wasn't interested in her, but he was oddly possessive. A guy thing, she figured. He'd staked his claim and she was his.

The crowd burst into applause, again. She especially loved this part, when he took it all in, accepting their praise with humility and grace. He stood perfectly still as he looked out to the audience, then to each of the team members within range. His final stop was a glance at her, followed by a wink and a nod. She then gave him a thumbs up. It had become their secret code of appreciation.

She never doubted that he believed in her. Even while she was still fighting the idea of being in Virginia and completely out of her depth. Those first few weeks were an exercise in degradation, with Stanley screaming all the time and her unable to find her own ass with two hands. But she rallied and got her shit together, with a double impetus of wanting to piss off Stanley and impress Connor.

He defended her from those few who didn't appreciate her meteoric rise in the campaign. He was always kind and patient with her, even when he shouldn't have been. From those months together, she'd learned that patience was definitely not his strong suit. Not with anyone else. That, among many things, made him so hard to figure out. And so damn attractive. If only she could do something about those terrible suits. And the inconvenient feelings.

CHAPTER 7

The crowd kept chanting Connor's name. It had been a good speech. A good day.

Connor might not have had the most, or the loudest supporters, but he was certain he had the best. He caught another drop of sweat from his temple. It was one of the hottest days on record, especially since it wasn't even summer yet, and he'd still gotten a decent turnout.

As he did after every event, he spent the final moments making eye contact with as many people in the audience as possible. Then, to his staff members, and finally to the woman who was glowing even more than usual. That blonde hair, pulled tight, was like a miniature sun. Right there, a few feet away from him.

He waited for at least half the people to stop clapping before walking off the stage. One of the few things he'd learned from Stanley that he hadn't had to erase from his brain.

The split with his crazed campaign manager had most likely tanked his campaign. Not that he'd been doing that well before, anyway, as all the conflicting messages left the population of Virginia confused, at best, and unhappy at worst. But at least, Stanley was gone now, and Connor could run the rest of his campaign, short as it might turn out to be, with integrity.

Yeah, he was almost certainly not going to survive past the primaries. The combination of the Stanley debacle and growing anti-Barrett sentiment kept him near the bottom of the small pile of candidates. The only reason he'd even lasted that long was his secret weapon. His Golden Girl. Not that he'd ever dare call her that to her face. He had no doubt that Jenna King would deck him with her small, bony fist. He wasn't going to take his chances. She was tough.

At that moment, she was standing under a tree barely providing enough shade for her tall silhouette. The smile on her face outshone even the dazzling day.

After a nod of her head, she began to walk toward the tent. He fell into pace next to her.

"Nice job, Barrett. Sharp speech. Love the new jokes. Great work making everyone feel appreciated, which was good considering they all braved heatstroke to come out here and support you."

"Thanks, Jenna. And please stop calling me Barrett." He'd told her that a million times.

She handed him a towel. "Okay, dry off, then you've got about twenty minutes to meet-n-greet. You've got the Bill Powers radio show in half an hour, but you can do that from the car on the way back to the hotel."

Before he could respond, she twisted the cap off his water bottle and handed it to him. "Drink. Don't want you getting dehydrated."

He quirked a smile as they entered the tent. "Yes, boss."

She stopped, put her hands on her hips and stared straight ahead. It was always hard to tell whether she had someone talking to her through the headset. A slow blink let him know exactly where her attention was. "We don't have time for your sarcasm, Barrett. Now, don't save the world all in one go, okay?" Which was her code for, make the conversations quick. They had somewhere to be.

Someone pulled the sweaty towel from his hand and he turned to walk back out onto the fairgrounds. But not before watching Jenna stride across the tent. Like a mother duck, with every step, a few more of her babies got in line and followed her. Watching her do her thing was one of his favorite parts of this otherwise grueling endeavor. And, of course, the rear view was spectacular.

Connor had stopped beating himself up about his inappropriate thoughts. He wanted her, sure. Could even admit he had feelings for her. But he respected her more than anyone he'd ever met, and, given their current positions, that would have to take precedence. Boning his campaign manager was always on his mind, but could never actually happen.

Maybe he'd have a chance with Jenna in the future. For now, he'd have to wait. The final debate before the primaries was in two days and he needed to be laser-focused on his goal.

He walked back out and the applause began again. The adulation was wonderful, but having real conversations with the people of his state provided the fuel that made everything else work. It almost balanced out the madness. Big stages and booming applause were great. But witnessing another person's desire to improve their life or their county or their country was the whole reason he wanted to do this crazy thing. With every handshake, with every sincere question, heck even every baby he had to kiss, his certainty grew.

He wanted this. As much as he'd ever wanted anything in his life. But the chances were less than slim. He hadn't blamed his staff for quitting when Stanley was in charge. He could barely stand the man. But it had left him screwed. Thank God for Jenna, who not only moved across the country for him, but took up the mantle of leadership as if it had been hers all along.

The straggling staff lined up behind her, and she recruited more in no time. Maybe if he'd had the balls to fire Stanley earlier, they would've had enough time to make up for the disruption. But it left them too far behind.

He was still young. He could run again next election. Write this one off to poor personnel choices. Either way, he was going to finish this out with his head high and knowing exactly how he would do it next time. Without a doubt there would be a next time.

As Jenna predicted, he'd lingered too long and found her sweet-talking the radio host while he jumped in the limo. "Sorry," he mouthed while she handed him the campaign phone.

Nothing new there. He could swear that all the TV and radio talk show hosts shared the same script of ridiculous questions. They all wanted to spend half of the precious minutes talking about his dating life, who he'd been seen with, what he ate for breakfast. What had happened to people that the important stuff didn't even make it on their radar?

He hung up the call and before he could catch his breath, Jenna held out her personal phone. "Aunt Olivia."

Not the first person he was interested in talking to, but he knew avoiding her wouldn't work. Jenna's aunt and uncle, who'd been like parents to him, had started calling her when they wanted to reach him. Probably figured out that she'd make sure to get him on the phone. "Hi, Aunt Olivia."

"I saw you on TV, darling. You looked good. A bit overheated, but good."

That was about as complimentary a greeting as he could expect. "Thanks. It was blazing out there today."

"Yes." She cleared her throat. "I'm sure you're terribly busy, but I want to remind you about Uncle Robert's birthday."

"Of course. How could I forget?"

"Well..." Unsaid was the number of events he constantly 'forgot' because he just didn't want to go.

"I would never forget his birthday. I'll be there."

"Are you bringing Eleanor?"

He flitted eyes at Jenna, tapping away on her tablet as if she was composing a new constitution. "Uh... I'm not sure. Does it matter?"

"I need to know for headcount. And for Jenna, too. Is she bringing someone?"

He had no idea. "I'll find out."

"Fine, then."

"Love you. I'll talk to you soon."

He hung up and waited for Jenna to look up from her device. "Thanks for today. You handled a potentially tough day with grace, as always."

She gave him that half-smile that, had he not known her, might be mistaken for bashful self-consciousness. "Sorry for being so brusque about your shirt. Didn't mean to-"

"You were right." He gave her a small poke with his elbow. "And maybe I'm getting used to being man-handled."

Her eyebrows vaulted to her hairline.

"Kidding. What happened to your sense of humor today?"

She shook her head. "So much on my mind."

He understood. She was trying her damndest to resuscitate a half-dead campaign. He wished he could do something nice for her, but she rebuffed him every time he tried. And he had to watch himself. It would be easy to lavish her with praise and gifts. She deserved it all. But he needed to manage the perception of their relationship.

They sat silently for the remaining minutes of the car ride. He looked out the window at the lush landscape streaming past. The city felt so far away from here, the rolling hills of the countryside softening into a haze of green. Heat and excitement still coursed through him, but with every tree, every wildflower-filled field, his body relaxed. Just as important as gearing up for big events, was the coming down. Staying too hyped up, for too long, was a recipe for disaster.

He let a flicker of worry pass. It had been a long time since anxiety had punctured his life, but he had to stay diligent with his practices. Otherwise, he'd find himself back to his teenage years—out of control and out of his mind.

He kept count to his breaths, stretching them out longer with each round. Deep breathing, meditation, and his daily ass-kicking workouts kept him in fighting shape, free from old demons. Despite the utter exhaustion of his body, he was itching for the hard run he'd take when they arrived at the hotel.

Jenna's phone buzzed and she scowled, thumbs moving so fast across the screen, her long fingers blurred. He imagined what it would be like to surprise her with a kiss. She'd look up at him with those eyes that usually transmitted fierce determination which would instead be filled with softness and love. He could see it so clearly in his head, as if the alternate Universe was as real as the one around him. *Snap out of it, Con.*

His stomach grumbled. "Hey, what are we doing for dinner?"

Without looking up from her phone, she answered. "Luisa's got something set up. Not sure what, but we'll eat in my suite during the meeting."

"I'm going out for a run, first. Want to take advantage of the cooler temperature."

"You already went running this morning!" she answered, with fake exasperation and that look that made it seem like her big blue eyes were cartoon-sized.

He held eye contact until she looked away.

"Fine," she huffed. "But you need to come back in less than an hour. No marathons."

Nothing could keep the smile from taking over his face. "Deal."

Their game was fun. He'd never enjoyed getting bossed around as much as he had with her. All that stuff Jackson had said about her had at first seemed accurate, but was now irrelevant. She had taken charge. Fully and completely. Everyone was polite enough to acknowledge his position, but it was clear who was running things. Not that he ever wanted to deny her anything, but something about Jenna King made the word 'no' fall out of his vocabulary.

When he finally made it to her room, everyone had already gathered. The casual conversations slowed as he took his seat on the small couch next to her. Jenna had taken off her shoes, but other than her bare feet, was as put together as she'd been all day. He was freshly showered after a run he resented having to cut short, full of energy, and ready for the night. At least, ready to be sitting inches away from her for as long as he could.

CHAPTER 8

*E*very time Jenna glanced at Connor, his eyelids seemed heavier. The debrief had, hours later, turned into a planning brainstorm. Gabe and Daniel, their publicist, sat at the small table with their laptops. Luisa took the upholstered chair, her notepad perched on her perfectly crossed legs, while Jenna and Connor shared the loveseat.

She knew he'd needed to go for that run earlier, but maybe it had been too much. He looked utterly depleted. A quick nap would have probably been a better idea for him, as if he'd ever agree to that in a million years.

The rest of the crew also looked tired. All but Luisa, whose eyes still sparkled as if it was midday instead of midnight. They weren't done plotting out their final points for the debate—less than a day away now—but maybe some rest would do them all some good. Especially Connor.

He startled when she touched his shoulder. "Hey, you. Why don't we call it a night?"

She'd meant to whisper, but everyone's eyes snapped to her.

"We're not done yet," Gabe said. "We need to get those talking points agreed on and tested before Monday."

This was the new politics, where everything was crowd-sourced and tested before launch. Jenna hated ruling by committee.

"Connor needs to rest." She winced at how that made her sound like his mother. Or his wife. "And so do you guys. I can see the wear-and-tear."

"We're fine," offered Daniel.

She looked from face to face, partially frustrated by their lack of agreement, and partially warmed by their dedication. She landed on Connor's tired face last. He needed to sleep. Nothing worked if he wasn't on his game.

"I think you should go to bed," she said in as neutral as tone as she could. "We can finish up and we'll catch you up in the morning."

He shook his head.

"Connor, I don't need to remind you how important this debate is. *Please* go get some rest."

He shook his head harder and smiled. That fucker was enjoying watching her beg.

An idea popped into her head. "How about we all take a quick break? Use the bathroom, have a stretch, grab some water or coffee. Gabe, can you clean up those last two points and we'll go over them when we reconvene? Let's say, twenty minutes."

Gabe nodded without looking up from his computer, fingers moving briskly over the keys. "You got it, JK."

Jenna didn't love that nickname, but it wasn't the time to debate it. She wrapped her hand around Connor's arm, his bicep tightening under her grip. Damn. "You, go into my room and take one of your power naps. I'll wake you up when we start again."

Connor was well known among the group for his miraculous ability to fall into a deep sleep for a few minutes and wake up as if he'd been down for ten hours. And he could sleep anywhere—a loud meeting, a jostling car, even standing up while he was getting mic-ed up for media appearances. She'd never gotten the full story of his ability, but the rumor was he'd been trained by a Buddhist monk to attain the highest states of meditation.

She smiled to herself, imagining Connor with a shaved head and wearing nothing but saffron robes.

"Fine," he answered with a gravelly voice.

She watched as he walked the two steps to one of the doors of the suite and entered. Just as the door clicked close, Jenna realized how odd it was that he would be sleeping in her bedroom. She should have sent him to his own room.

A series of enticing images popped into her head. She and Connor had perfected their platonic relationship, but there was always something more for her. She didn't want to want him—no good could come from that—but it was getting harder to hold back. Tempting fate like this, publicly, was not a good idea. She looked around the room at her colleagues. No one else seemed to care, as evidenced by the non-reactions around her. It was too late to wake him up, anyway.

Craving some fresh air, she made her way out of the hotel, past a yawning desk attendant. It was a perfect night—warm with a cooler breeze and a sky full of stars. They were remote enough that the sky beamed, free of the artificial light of civilization. There were so many things about her new - and temporary - home that drove her crazy, but she had to admit that Virginia was growing on her.

As was her boss. Connor grew more impressive, and more attractive, with each passing day. Sometimes, he reminded her of her father, the most powerful man in her life. The kind of regal power she always looked for in the overly masculine men she'd dated. But they never had it, which she could tell because all their insecurity and fear eventually seeped out.

Connor had no issue acceding his control to her, without fear of his power being diminished. She noticed it from the moment she arrived at the campaign office. He listened and treated everyone with respect. If someone had a better idea than his, he welcomed it. He walked around the world as if he knew exactly who he was and what he was capable of. A masculinity more intoxicating than all the barrel chests and thick beards in the world.

Jenna took in a waft of magnolia blossoms before going back inside, trying to convince herself that all those feelings could be successfully tucked away. Even as she entered her room, she repeated under her breath, "Senator Connor Barrett," a reminder of the importance of her job and the impossibility of her desires.

When she opened the bedroom door a crack and heard the deep hush of his breath, she didn't have the heart to wake him up. He'd be mad at her in the morning, but she would deal with it. His rest and recovery was more important. They had all made an unspoken pact: Connor's success came first.

"All right, gang." She rubbed her hands together "Let's bust this out."

Eager faces lit around her and a rush of gratitude gripped the center of her chest.

AFTER ONLY FOUR hours of fitful sleep, Jenna didn't expect to feel as energized as she did. Sneaking out of bed and into the bathroom without making even the tiniest sound took all the self-control she could muster. It was much too reminiscent of past sexual encounters, even though her night hadn't had any action. She exhaled only after the bathroom door clicked shut.

The hot spray of a rainfall shower-head pulled a happy groan from her throat. It was always a wonderful surprise when mediocre hotel rooms had kick-ass showers. Thinking about the man on the other side of the bathroom door, still asleep in her bed, she drew her fingers between her legs for some relief.

The team had given her odd looks when she entered the room after the meeting, but at that point she was too tired to care. They were probably taking bets on whether she and Connor had slept together, but her professional demeanor would still any rumors. Hopefully, Connor wouldn't be weird about having shared a bed with her. Not that he even knew it had happened. He'd slept so hard, she'd checked his breathing more than once.

Clearing the steamy bathroom required cracking open the door. She needed the mirror to finish her hair and makeup so she could make it to her breakfast meeting with Gabe.

A finger cleared stray eyeliner from the edge of her eye. Her makeup routine had amped up a bit now that she was around adults all day instead of ungrateful kids, but she liked to keep it simple. Getting all her hair tucked away every morning took most of the time. The combination of the heat, humidity, and much more conservative aesthetic kept her mass of blonde waves out of sight.

It had taken some time to find clothes that communicated the right amount of professionalism and femininity, but she'd done it. Tailored slacks, skirts, blouses, and dresses were her daily choices. Her all-black outfits of skinny jeans and slouchy tops were well in her past. The only remnant of old Jenna was the tiny diamond piercing her left nostril.

The bed creaked as she placed the final bobby pin in the

large bun at the back of her head. She pushed the door open to find Connor sitting up and rubbing his eyes.

"Good morning, sleepyhead."

He yawned and ran his fingers through his hair, which fell immediately into place. He even woke up looking perfect. Geez. "It's morning."

She laughed at his disorientation. "Yes. I let you sleep. And it looks like you needed it."

"Did you sleep?" He turned and patted the other side of the bed. "Here?"

"Yes." She pointed across the room, to the opposite side of the King-sized bed. "All the way over there."

He tilted his head and smiled. She turned back to the mirror and picked up her tube of mascara. She needed to finish getting ready and he needed to stop looking at her like that.

"Well, another new experience for us."

She pressed her lips together. Why wasn't he rushing out to get himself ready for the day? "Yes. But no big deal. Right?"

She regretted the question as soon as it popped out of her mouth. Leaving it open for discussion meant more awkward minutes.

"I'm not sure I've ever slept with a woman. Without *sleeping* with a woman."

"Okay..."

He walked over to the doorway of the bathroom. She glanced at his crumpled but ridiculously sexy frame in the mirror before sweeping the mascara wand across her eyelashes.

"Are you attracted to me, Jenna?"

What the holy hell? There was no way she was entertaining this conversation. *Shut it down, Jenna.*

"Connor. I hope you know how much I respect you.

Admire you. How committed I am to getting you in the Senate. I'm here because I believe in you and I want to help you win."

"But not fuck?"

Her mascara wand bounced off the bathroom counter and made a perfect arc into the toilet.

She stared down at the black wand, the very expensive black wand, floating in the thankfully clean bowl. Her heart beat so hard her whole body pulsed.

She turned to find him leaning against the doorframe, arms crossed. Everything about her no-biggie plan came into question. She should have slept on the couch, or kicked him out to sleep in his own bed.

"What the hell, Connor? Why are you asking me that?"

He rubbed a finger across his lips. His full, sexy lips. Dammit. "Our relationship is extraordinary. Singular. We've spent nearly every day together for the past three months. We get along perfectly and never get sick of each other."

"Oh, I get sick of you plenty."

He laughed, which should have cut the tension, but only made her more uncomfortable.

"I've never had that. Especially not with a beautiful woman."

Irrelevant and inappropriate. "Why is that important?"

"Sometimes..." He cleared his throat. "I'm just not sure how you see me. You tell me what to say, what to do, when to do it, you even dress and undress me."

A glimmer of clarity appeared. He was just having a guy moment. Feeling insecure and wanting to exert his masculinity. Got it.

"Don't worry, I know you're a man, Connor. Your job is to show that to the people of Virginia." Good. Get the conversation back to business.

"Is it because I'm not a tough and beefy bad boy?"

Fuck, fuck, fuck. She took a step toward him, hoping he would move out of the doorway and she could get out of the bathroom. It was feeling much too close in there. He didn't budge. "Why would you say that?

He dropped his arms, slipping his hands in his pockets. "Maybe I heard whispers about your type."

That was the last straw. She put her palm on his chest and pushed him back, finally freed from her prison. "Listen, don't get distracted with this stuff. This is your career we're dealing with. Don't get confused in thinking you have to win some chase with me. Is a piece of ass really worth your future?"

He jerked back. "Did you just call yourself a piece of ass?"

"Dammit, Connor. We really don't have time for this." She slipped on her heels. "I don't know what's going on with you. Maybe you're over-tired or over-stressed. If you need some time off-"

"I don't need time off, Jenna." His entire demeanor shifted. Even his voice deepened, which she felt through the center of her body. "I'm trying to get a firmer grasp on our relationship. It's important that we're always clear. We're working so closely together that we can't afford ambiguity. Or any holes in our communication. I need to know where you stand."

His words slammed against her. He wasn't pursuing her. He was worried about her lusting after him. What a dick. She knew, definitively, that she'd given him no sign of her desire. How presumptuous to think that every woman in the world would be falling at his feet.

"What matters is that you keep your eye on the prize. You don't have to worry about me. I've always had mine on the right goal."

CHAPTER 9

*C*onnor hid the tremor in his body as she picked up her phone and room key, and stomped out of the room. The intensity of her exit sent him sitting back down on the bed. Well, that didn't go as planned. At all.

He ran his hand over the rumpled sheets where he'd slept, focusing on his breath. He had to calm down. A deep exhale sent his head into his hands. Crap.

The plan had sounded flawless in his head. As he lay awake—listening to the shower running and imagining her in there, water cascading over her body, his dick aching for her—he knew he had to say something. He needed to know if she felt anything when she'd gotten into bed with him. Her body that close to him, even though he wasn't even consciously aware of it, had amped up his typical assortment of sex dreams about Jenna. He must have been moaning all night.

Her reaction made it perfectly clear she had no interest. Which he should have expected. But it was still disappointing.

He glanced over at the clock. It was time to get on with the day. They'd be headed off to the local station before a

Town Hall meeting. Then the debate tomorrow. The one that would decide how badly he was going to lose the primaries.

HE ARRIVED AT HIS ROOM, stripped out of the clothes he was still wearing from the day before, and dropped to the ground. A hundred pushups and situps later, only a small amount of his agitation had been worked off. When he stepped under the cold water coming out of the shower, the pain felt deserved.

What a fucking idiot he was, thinking he'd sensed some tenderness from her. *Still clueless about women, Connor.* And now, she was probably furious with him and he'd have to grovel for forgiveness. Which he didn't mind doing, but he hated that he might have really offended her. That was the last thing he wanted.

Even the cold water did nothing to relieve the aching tightness around his balls. He soaped up his right hand and got to work, not even trying to push the images of Jenna out of his mind.

CONNOR WALKED into the hotel restaurant feeling only slightly better. Most of the team sat around a large table, eating and laughing. They all stopped as he approached, and he definitely didn't imagine the strange looks. They thought something had happened. He wondered how he was going to clear that up, but that was a secondary issue. He needed to find her.

Sitting on the same side of a small table, she and Gabe were in the middle of a serious conversation. Or so it appeared by the looks on their faces, so close to each other they could almost be kissing. He stopped in his tracks. Was something going on between them? Gabe was a committed player, but he figured bro-code would keep his hands off her.

Connor clenched his jaw. He kept forgetting he had no claim on Jenna. She wasn't his girlfriend, she was his employee. Which meant that Gabe probably wouldn't know she was off limits. Fuck. How had he not known this was going on?

Deep breath, man. Maybe it was for the best. If she hooked up with Gabe, then he could more easily get over his ridiculous infatuation. Hopefully.

He looked around the crowded restaurant for an empty table.

"Connor! Hey, Connor!" Gabe's voice boomed across the room.

Connor met his friend's wave and tried to evade Jenna's scowl. There was no avoiding them now. "Good morning."

Gabe put out his hand, which he slapped. "Hey, I heard you slept like a dead guy. That's good, man. You need to recharge your batteries."

He glanced at Jenna, wondering how much she had shared with Gabe. Embarrassment warmed his throat. "Yeah, I slept like a baby. Ready to kill it today."

"Awesome! Go grab some breakfast and sit down. JK and I have nailed the final talking points. You're going to love 'em."

He hated how Gabe called her JK, as if she was some teenage tomboy. Or a wizard-writing British writer. Her name was Jenevieve, which he'd looked up. It meant an incredibly spirited person with a wicked temper but beautiful soul, which was perfect for her. He walked toward the buffet with disgust superseding hunger, and filled his plate regardless.

SHE WAS STANDING when he returned to the table, with

Gabe's hand around her wrist.

"I'm going to head up, finish a few things. You two can handle it from here," she said.

Gabe tugged on her arm. "No. You should stay. You're always the voice of reason."

She looked from one man to the other, her expression not entirely pleased, then sat back down.

Gabe flipped open his laptop as Connor shoveled a few large bites of egg into his mouth.

"I feel like I've got stronger comebacks for the whole Barrett-hate faction. But I need to make sure you're okay with them."

Connor dropped his fork. "Seriously? Aren't people tired of talking about my family? It's not like I had anything to do with my grandfather's governing, or even my uncles. I'm not another version of them."

Gabe typed away. "We know that, man, but you know... people. Gotta address the issues, not just proclaim that they're unreasonable. And that name of yours might be calling the critics, but it's come with some perks, too."

Connor speared a piece of melon, imagining Gabe's face under the tines of his fork. "I understand that I have benefitted from being a Barrett. I just think there are more important things to address, like my policies, for instance."

Jenna had been looking away for the entire conversation, but turned to him and met his gaze. Finally. "You're right, Connor. But it's your job to steer the conversation. It's not their job to only bring up the topics you want to talk about."

Gabe wrapped his arm around her shoulders and pulled her even closer. "See? This is why we needed you to stay. Dropping the wisdom bombs."

Connor thought melon would eject out of his face. "Got it."

"Okay, check this out."

Gabe read from his computer while Connor pretended to listen. All he could take in was Gabe's thick fingers squeezing Jenna's shoulder.

BY THE TIME he and Jenna were in the car, riding to the radio station, the switch had been reset. She was in full campaign manager mode, speaking into her headset and tapping on her tablet. He stared out the window and chewed on his lower lip. Tension still trickled between them and he couldn't stand it. Whatever it took, he was going to make it right.

Alex pulled the car into a loading zone in front of an old brick building. He exited and opened Jenna's door for her. She looked up at him and smiled. "Oh, sorry Alex. I'll be staying in the car. Maybe we can find a decent coffee while Connor's doing the interview."

The older man bowed his head and walked to Connor's side. When the door opened, Connor shook off the shock at Jenna's announcement and checked his watch. "I need a minute, Alex. Thanks."

The door closed and Alex stayed outside. He'd understood Connor's shorthand for private conversation.

Jenna was watching him with squinted eyes, devices in her hands. "What are you doing?"

He rotated his body to face her. "I'd like to talk about what happened. This morning."

She waved the hand holding her phone and shook her head. "We don't have to. It's fine."

He slid closer. "No. It's not. I'm sorry. What I did was completely inappropriate. I don't know what I was thinking. All that sleep muddled my brain. I can't believe I said what I did."

Her bright blue eyes took him in. That gaze could melt anyone's resolve, but he was determined. "I need to know that everything's okay between us. What we're doing is so hard that it becomes impossible if," he said while pointing between them, "we're not working. I can't do it, Jenna."

Something in her face shifted, but it happened so quickly he didn't have time to decipher it.

"I think we need to be careful, Connor. With our words *and* our actions. It's just too easy for our relationship to be misconstrued and it's important that it not be. For the sake of your campaign."

As usual, she was right. It wasn't what he wanted to hear, but she'd made herself clear. That line wouldn't be crossed again. "I understand. I'll keep my insecurities to myself in the future."

Her face expressed the disbelief he was feeling on the inside. Fuck, fuck, fuck. "Okay, sorry, let me rephrase. What I meant to say is that if I'm having some random thought that's not relevant or appropriate, I'm going to keep it to myself. I don't ever want to make you feel uncomfortable."

That was hardly a recovery and he could see it on her horrified expression. He would need to get a better grip on what was coming out of his mouth if he didn't want to also blow this interview.

She looked down at her phone. "You need to go. It's time."

"Right," he said, reluctantly. What a crappy moment to have to cut a conversation. Or maybe the forced ending would keep him from stuffing his foot any further down his throat.

"Break a tooth." She forced a smile.

At least she remembered their secret pre-interview salute. He shook his head all the way into the building. Maybe he should hope for an early end to his campaign. He'd just messed up the best thing about it.

CHAPTER 10

"*I* mean, what the actual fuck?" Jenna paced around her small living room and flipped her palms up as if she was imploring the heavens for an explanation. She was still in her pajamas, hair wild, anger coursing through her a full twenty-four hours after the hotel incident. All those messages had convinced Camille to come over first thing in the morning and help her sort out the recent mess.

Camille's face had shifted from shock to horror and back over the course of the story. "Whoa, babe. I thought Jackson and I were dramatic. You've taken it to another level."

Hands went to hips. "First of all, you and my annoying brother were not just dramatic. You were completely stupid. For ten years. It's only been a few months with Connor. And it's a totally different situation."

Camille perched forward on the couch. "Agreed. You're colleagues. But Jen, he asked if you wanted to fuck him. I seriously can't think of a single reasonable thing to say about that. I might have smacked him."

"Except for the fact that I *want* to fuck him. But I can't."

Camille's eyes flitted from side to side. Jenna knew there

wasn't an easy solution but she hoped her best friend would have something helpful to say. If Camille didn't have an answer, there probably wasn't one.

"What's the worse thing that would happen? I mean, if you did."

Jenna groaned. "Plenty. He might find out who I really am. Besides, I think he's only thinking about it because I'm probably the only woman in his life who hasn't thrown herself at him. So, I think sleeping with him would mean the end of all respect for me. Personally *and* professionally. I mean, would you take the woman who was sleeping with the boss seriously? I'm sure the boss wouldn't."

Camille shook her head. "He really doesn't seem like a player. Or a dick. I'd be surprised if he was only into the chase and catch."

"Then how do you explain what he said?" Frustration pitched her voice much higher than she wanted.

"Maybe he picked up a vibe from you and wanted to confirm before he made his move."

No way. "I was giving no vibe. And before that moment, he'd never gone anywhere near that topic."

"I don't know, sweets. I wish I had a better answer for you."

"Me too. The past day has been so painful. I'm hyper-analyzing everything he's doing and everything I'm doing and it's exhausting."

"How about Gabe? Can he take your mind off all this? He's clearly interested, right?"

"Yeah." At least that part was unambiguous. Gabe regularly made advances. They were smooth and skilled, but not subtle. "He's not trying to hide that he's a player. But at least it's all up front. I know where I stand. With Connor, I'm holding some line which is more than likely all about my feelings, not his."

Camille picked at her thumbnail, the sign she had lost herself in thought. Or worry. "Are you attracted to Gabe?"

"Yeah. He's hot. But I'm not trying to score. It's strictly flirty fun." She twisted her lips. "I'm not sure it was such a good idea to ask him to accompany me to Uncle Robert's party. I can sense that he and Connor have some competitive thing going on and I don't need to set up another tense situation. All I need right now is them going all caveman on me."

"Isn't Connor bringing some woman? Aunt Olivia told me it's one of his *dates*." Camille made air quotes.

Jenna pretended to gag. Connor's matchmaking candidates had been a source of contention between them, but she'd decided silence was her best strategy. Seeing him with someone else wasn't going to be the best feeling ever, but it was necessary. Connor as an object of infatuation would have to be completely erased from her mind.

"I've got a theoretical."

Jenna sat on the couch with a grunt. Camille had always been insightful, but now that she and Jackson had become inseparable, she absorbed even more of his psychological brilliance. Through a made-up situation, she often found a way to untangle a complex issue. Jenna just didn't feel like playing.

"What if he has feelings for you?"

"Gabe? No way. He's strictly a horizontal prospect."

"No, I mean Connor."

Jenna had been forcing that idea out of her mind since the beginning. It would swallow her whole, preventing her from doing the job she was committed to doing. She clutched her stomach.

This adventure—moving across the country and the campaign—had been so far outside of her experience, she might as well have signed up for a trip to Mars. It had been the boldest thing she'd done in her entire life. But it was based on an ideal and a vision. It couldn't come down to her falling for Connor. Or him falling for her. It just couldn't. "Cammy, I don't want to go there. My sole focus needs to be him in that beautiful building down the road. It can't be that I did all this for some hot guy."

Camille tsked. "Avoidance is not your friend, here. You are already thinking about him this way, so might as well address it. Maybe then, you could do your job even better."

"Impossible." Jenna thought about how far they'd come. "I'm killing it."

Camille poked her in the shoulder. "I know you are. But back to the question. What would happen if his interest was legitimate?"

Jenna shook out her hair and ran her fingers through it. Wearing her hair up all the freaking time had taken a toll on her scalp. "It would never work. This is his life, his dream, not mine. Even if we don't win, he *will* end up in the Senate eventually. And maybe even in the White House. You and I both know that I don't fit in either of those places."

"I don't agree with you at all. Maybe old Jenna. But new, improved bad-ass boss babe Jenna would make Jackie O look like a slacker. Seriously. My only issue with you being First Lady is that it's not high enough."

"See, now I know you're tripping. I have no desire for that."

"So why not consider being with him?"

"You know, his primary criterion for the women his match-maker sends him is that they're White-House-ready."

Camille made the bad-smell face Jenna expected to see.

"Part of me wants to barf. And part of me thinks it's cool that he knows what he wants. And he's planning ahead."

"Regardless, there's no way I would qualify. You know my past, my history."

"Yes, I do. You think he doesn't have a bunch of stuff he regrets?"

That would be impossible. "No way. He's so straight-laced. Like, I doubt he's ever bounced a check. Even by accident. Connor lives his life around a code that's never been broken, as far as I can tell."

"I think that's what he allows the world to see. Just like you show different parts of you to different people. It doesn't make you unworthy. It makes you human."

Damn. Her heart leapt with gratitude that she had a friend who knew all of her. Had seen so much of the bad stuff with her own eyes and never wavered. It would be foolish to think Connor could be the same, but how wonderful that would be.

"I just don't think he could handle all of it. All of me."

"I don't know if he can, either. But it's the first time I've ever heard you talk about the possibility. Could you see yourself being completely honest with him? Not hiding anything?"

No, no, no. This conversation was going in the wrong direction. "I think the more I reveal everything that's inside me, the further I am from what he's looking for. It's more like Lindsay Lohan then Jackie O in there."

"I think that's exactly what he likes about you, babe."

Jenna sighed with exasperation. "I'm done with this theoretical. It's not worth thinking about. Too far fetched. Too impossible. And just a diversion from what I'm here to do. I didn't upend my life to get a guy. There were plenty back in San Francisco."

"I know that. Just because it wasn't about that doesn't mean it can't be an added bonus."

"The election is too important to me. I'm all in on the Connor-for-Senate train. I might even be driving that train. There's only one finish line. Period."

Camille pulled her in for a hug. "Okay, love. I have no doubt you're going to make it happen."

JENNA WAS happy to flip the conversation to Camille's upcoming wedding. It was going to be in late September in Sonoma Valley, Jackson and Camille's favorite place. Jenna felt bad that she hadn't been more available to her best friend. It was a momentous occasion for both of them. Her brother and her best friend, after a decade, had finally admitted their love. No one was happier about it then Jenna. Well, maybe they were happier, but Jenna was definitely number three. She'd have to carve out some more time to support Camille.

The idea hit her that her whole adventure in politics might come to a screeching halt in one week, which would give her plenty of time for wedding planning. But it was the last thing she wanted. Connor had to win the primary, even though it was a long shot at this point. To do that, he needed a decisive win in the debate, which would be happening in less than eight hours. And that's exactly why imagining him loving her was all wrong. As she constantly reminded him: eye on the prize.

BY THE END of the morning, Jenna had gone over the situation with Connor so many times, it had brought a pounding to her temples. But it had made several things clear:

1. She couldn't lead Gabe on, even if it would relieve some of the ever-building frustration.

2. She needed more time away from Connor. All that proximity was causing her focus to blur.

3. She would stop pretending her feelings weren't there. She'd just have to get better at managing them.

All the focus on the tall, hot man left her with a consuming desire to get to her phone. She had demanded that he take a mental health morning, which she was pretty sure he spent at the gym. It was the first morning they hadn't spent together in a really long time. She wanted to see him, hear him, make sure he was doing all right and not wracked with anxiety. She had no idea what he'd been thinking that morning in her room, but she knew it worried him. And that couldn't continue. He needed to be in top shape. So much depended on those few hours tonight.

She picked up her phone and stared at it.

"Just call him, already," Camille said as she came out of the bathroom.

There was no point asking her how she knew. They had the whole psychic thing nailed down.

The phone rang enough times that she figured he wasn't picking up. Maybe still working out.

"Hey!" a breathless voice boomed through the line.

"Oh, you're there. I was..." She swallowed. "Just wanted to make sure you're having a good morning."

"Yeah, went for a run with Lucas and then did the stadium stairs. It was awesome."

Her body relaxed at the sound of his voice. "Good."

"How are you doing? Holding up?"

"Yeah. Cammy's been hanging with me, so..." What could she say? They'd been talking about him nonstop?

"Oh, I'm glad she's there with you. Probably a welcome change of pace from my ugly mug."

If only he knew how far from ugly she found his mug. "Well, some girl time was a good thing."

"I'm glad, Jenna. But it felt weird not seeing you."

God, why did he have to say that? Yes, yes, a million times yes. "Well, you'll see *my* ugly mug in just a few hours."

"Yeah." His breathing was slowing, but still audible. She wondered what expression was on his face.

"Okay, then. See you later. Don't forget to eat."

"Ha!"

They both knew how disciplined he was about regular meals. That lean frame had no fat reserves. *Stop thinking about his body!* "You too."

Although her stomach was all grumbles and cramps, she would have to eat something, too. She headed into the kitchen after hanging up, a surprising rush of tears dropping her into her best friend's open arms.

CHAPTER 11

*C*onnor stood outside Jenna's front door, his heart racing and his confidence fading. Maybe this was inappropriate. Things were just starting to feel normal after his colossal fuck-up. He'd been giving her a bit more space than usual, keeping everything strictly professional, but it was killing him. Now that his win at the debate gave him a chance in the primaries, all he wanted to do was share his excitement. With her.

His certainty that he'd never make it this far in the election had imploded with the media's glowing attention. All of a sudden, he'd become the darling of the race. He couldn't attribute all of it to his performance at the debate. More likely the vagaries of people's preferences. Or the alignment of the planets.

He switched the six-pack of Jenna's favorite beer from one hand to the other. He was sweating. This was ridiculous. They were adults and if she didn't want to see him, she would say so. She probably wasn't even home, anyway. Probably out with her friends at some dark bar full of burly men.

He hoped she was home. It was six days until the

primaries and he wanted to be with her. Needed to talk to her about some ideas he had. She was the only one who would understand. He raised his hand and knocked twice.

At exactly the moment he considered knocking again, the door opened. And there she stood.

A surprised smile graced her face. "Hey."

"Hi, Jenna. I'm sorry for just showing up, but I had the most amazing idea. About courting the rural folks. I brought beer." He looked over her shoulder and noticed beer bottles on her coffee table and a set of legs. Men's legs.

"Shit! You have company. Oh my gosh, I'm so sorry. I really should have called first."

"Hey, is Lucas here with the food yet? I'm starving." A female voice came from behind Jenna before the door swung open.

Camille joined Jenna in the entryway, sharing an equally surprised expression. "Connor? It's you."

"Yeah, sorry. I didn't realize you were having a-"

"Don't be ridiculous." Jackson joined them in the increasingly crowded entryway. "Glad to have you. Come on in."

Connor checked Jenna's face. The surprise hadn't passed. He walked in anyway.

He received a warm hug from Camille, followed by a back slap from Jackson. Connor hadn't realized they were still in town. Probably hanging around for Robert's party that weekend.

After putting the beer down, he stood behind an overstuffed chair and shoved his hands in his pockets. They were all looking at him. *Awkward.*

"What are you wearing?" Jenna asked, head tilted like a confused puppy.

It was like one of those dreams where you arrived at a

party and realized you'd forgotten to get dressed. He looked down at his ratty AC/DC t-shirt and his favorite threadbare jeans. At least he wasn't naked. "Uhhh... just clothes for hanging out at home, I guess."

He lifted his gaze to her, ready to comment on her casual outfit, but in fact she was as impeccably dressed as always. Did this woman ever let her hair down?

"I like it," Jackson said. "It's nice to see you relaxed, like a regular guy."

"Me, too," Camille added with a nod. "You look great, Connor. Don't let Jenna give you any shit."

Attention on Jenna, he waited for the promised shit, but she said nothing. Just stared. Thankfully, the next knocks on the door took everyone's attention off him.

Ramona and Lucas walked right in, arms loaded with bags he recognized from Lucas' restaurant. "Hello, hello! Food's here!" They both whipped their heads toward Connor.

"Hey, Con! What are you doing here?" his best friend asked. Lucas put the large bags down on the coffee table. He ran the hottest restaurants in town and had been keeping Connor well fed for years.

Connor wasn't aware that they'd all become hangout buddies. He tried to suppress the feeling of being left out. "Crashing a party, apparently."

His sister gave him a lingering hug. "Glad to see you, Con."

Lucas wrapped himself around the two of them. "It's my favorite Barrett sandwich."

Camille reached inside one of the bags and pulled out a rectangular container. "Oh my God, that smells so good, Lucas. I'm about to chew Jackson's arm off."

"I'll give you something else to nibble on, my darling." The room erupted in a series of groans as Connor stood mesmerized by the intimacy he had no idea existed. Sure, Camille and his sister had gotten close while working on the children's center. And Jackson and Lucas were cousins. So maybe it made sense that they were all so chummy. But still...

Jenna touched his arm, startling him out of his daze. "This is not going to be a G-rated evening. I hope that's all right."

Did she think he was some kind of prude? He decided to let go of the lingering slight and enjoy the unexpected party. "I'm happy to be here."

By the time they'd all had too much food, and an impressive amount of beer, Connor had nearly forgotten why he'd shown up at Jenna's place.

Ramona, who was turning out to be the poster child for pregnancy, all glowing and happy, put down her sparkling water. "So, how was it that you got my brother out of his mancave, and his suit, to hang out with us?"

He scowled at his sister. "Super not fair, Mo."

Jenna shrugged and grinned. "Actually, he just showed up at the door." Her eyes grew wide. "Oh my God, you came here to tell me something. About the campaign, right?"

It didn't seem important anymore. This was turning out to be one of the most fun and relaxed evenings he'd had in a long time. "Well, yeah, but I don't want to bore everyone. It's strategy stuff." He waved his arm and took another swig of beer.

Jackson sat forward. "Actually, I'd love to hear it. Politics fascinates me. It's nothing short of psychological warfare. My favorite."

Connor scanned all the eager faces in the room. Even Jenna was smiling and nodding. He stood up and described his idea for increasing his numbers in the outlying areas of the state, where his opponent had been dominating. It applied his plan for job creation directly toward the economic depression of the area.

The conversation twisted and turned, taking them late into the night. Lucas shared his experience serving the DC elite, Camille, the tech wiz, helped them crunch numbers and Jackson helped profile all the communities he would serve as Senator. It was as if Connor was given a rapid-fire doctorate in strategy, influence, and leadership. Jenna scribbled away in one of her notebooks, but remained relatively quiet.

He was awed by what had just happened. "You guys are amazing. I don't even know what to say."

Lucas patted him on the back. "We're all here for you and we believe in you. I mean, look at Jenna. Came all the way here to help you get elected."

His breath caught. That was no exaggeration. She'd sacrificed everything to work her ass off for him. He beamed at her, sitting on the far end of the couch, long legs curled under herself, all the fierceness of her normal expression transformed into a sweetness he could hardly resist. He closed his eyes to compose himself. "What's funny about that is how many times she refused me. I made every pitch in the book. She wasn't going to budge. Even Ramona and Jackson both tried. I think she agreed just to get us to shut up and leave her alone."

Everyone laughed.

"And then she shows up and takes over the place. I don't think people even knew she was an intern. From the moment she walked in the door, people assumed she was in charge. Now that's a kind of power I aspire to. And I know the campaign would have been dead months ago without her."

He raised his beer in her direction. Their eyes met and held, as if no one else was in the room.

"There's one more thing we need to discuss."

His sister's voice pulled his attention from the only person he wanted to be paying attention to. "What's up, Mo?"

"You need to up your fashion game."

Gasps filled the room.

"I hate to say this, Con, but you dress like an eighty-year-old man. You're a good-lucking guy who spends infinite hours working out and then you show up in these terrible suits. I think you should get Jackson to take you shopping or something."

Now, that was embarrassing. "Thanks, sis. I'm trying to eradicate poverty and you're interested in how my suits fit."

Jackson was the first to break the uncomfortable silence. "I really don't want to get in the middle of this, but it's well known that the visual component of influence is huge. Almost no place more than in politics, unfortunately."

"I have to agree, Con." Lucas gave him an apologetic smile.

Great. Even his best friend thought he dressed like a shlub.

"I'd be happy to take you," Jackson said. "But I've got a better idea. You should go with Jenna."

As if a paralytic agent had filled the room, no one moved. Jenna scowled at her brother.

"I'm not sure leather chaps and a dog collar are going to work for Connor," Camille said, breaking the tension.

Jackson spoke after the laughter had quieted. "That's funny, babe. But seriously, Jenna's got a great sense of style and you both are tall, thin physical types. She knows how to make that work."

Yes, her long, sleek body was stunning. He'd never seen her wear anything that wasn't flattering. Ever.

Ramona grabbed his forearm. "You can go to a mall in a district where you're dominating. Invite the media."

Jackson's face lit up. "The whole thing would make a great photo op. It would show you in a casual environment, where you're a bit self-deprecating and funny. Let your community see you in a different light." He swept his hand across an imaginary billboard. "Shop with Connor."

WHILE EVERYONE CHUCKLED at Jackson's crazy idea, Connor focused on the shock across Jenna's face. She might not have blinked.

"Great suggestion, Jackson, but I couldn't ask Jenna to do this. Especially since I'm apparently so fashion stunted."

Her lips twitched as she looked down. Then those big blue eyes beamed straight at him. "I want to."

His jaw dropped at Jenna's three quiet words. He couldn't believe what he'd just heard. They were only talking about going to a shopping mall, but something about the way she said it caused his heart to pound. It almost sounded as if she was agreeing to something completely different. Something that wouldn't require any clothes at all.

CHAPTER 12

*J*enna had never gotten this dressed up to go shopping. Ever.

The small photo op had turned into a huge media event, with several news stations and political bloggers sending film crews and photographers to follow them around. There was even a rumor that a New York fashion magazine was coming for a story she'd heard referred to as Mayor Makeover.

As Connor shopped for new threads, he'd also be hanging with his constituents. Jackson and Ramona had been right. It was a perfect plan, sure to deal the final blow to his remaining contenders and get him the nomination. It was going to be well worth her temporary discomfort.

This was the first time she'd be featured so prominently. She'd done plenty of radio interviews and even a few TV spots, but it was all from the neck up and a matter of one or two minutes. This could go on for hours, and cameras would be capturing every single thing. Even if she wasn't the one they'd come to see. As if helping him buy clothes wasn't going to be difficult enough - that body in and out of shirts and pants and jackets. Oy.

Jenna fiddled with the simple necklace that landed at the hollow of her throat. A single small diamond her father had bought her when she'd gotten into Princeton. "Grades before boys," he'd made her promise.

She had very few attachments to jewelry, or any stuff, but this piece made her feel his love and support. Made her remember that there were people who believed she could do anything. Despite all the bad that had come before.

The necklace didn't look right with the asymmetrical neckline of the fitted cream dress everyone insisted she wore. With nude stilettos, it made the perfect cool yet conservative statement, supposedly. Her brother was adamant that she look elegant and unfussy. As if she had just thrown it on and hadn't spent hours agonizing and preparing. Maybe she'd try something else on, just to see if it worked better.

The ring of the doorbell nipped that plan in the bud. Connor, in a light blue dress shirt and baggy, pleated pants, stood at her door. Even behind his glasses, she could see his eyes widen.

"Wow. You look great."

She stepped out of her house and walked toward the waiting car. "Thanks."

They had chosen one of the fancier malls in the suburbs north of the city. She settled in for the ride, trying not to notice how intently Connor was starting at her.

"Jenna, are you nervous?"

She looked down at her fidgeting hands then up at him. "Yeah. I guess I am."

He took both her hands in his. The feeling of being enveloped by his large, warm hands was immediately calming.

"What's going on? I don't remember ever seeing you nervous before."

"Well, this is the most front and center I've been. There are going to be cameras following my every move. What if I make a weird face, or say something stupid?"

He swallowed, as if he was nervous too, which she knew was impossible. "You're a natural. The camera loves you and I've yet to see you ever make a weird face or say something stupid. We both know which one of us is more likely to screw up."

She wove her fingers through his. He squeezed, which sent a quiver up her spine. Not trying to make it any bigger a deal than it was, she sat back in her seat and looked straight ahead. But she sure as hell didn't let go of that hand.

THE MEDIA HAD SWARMED the mall entrance by the time they arrived. Alex pulled the car over and turned off the engine.

Connor loosened his grip on Jenna's fingers. Yes, no more holding hands.

"The new buttons came in." He pulled a small round button with Barrett for Senate from the cupholder.

"Oh, cool!" They looked great. Of course, Luisa, who'd taken over much of their design work, had done a great job.

He held it close to her chest. "May I?"

If she could have forced her blood to stop running through her veins in order to avoid the blush in her cheeks, she would have. "Yes, thanks."

His long fingers moved so slowly, she wondered if he was concerned about touching her. So gently, he pinched a piece of fabric above her heart and slid the pin through. Everything was so close it nearly hurt. His face inches from hers, his hands almost touching her breast, those eyes burning into her.

Jenna was certain that the temperature of the car had risen at least ten degrees. She tried not to take too deep of a breath, which would bring her chest even closer to him. Her eyes slid up to watch his face as he concentrated on the small task of pinning the button to her dress. A feeling pressed against the back of her throat and she swallowed, hard, against it.

As if he knew what she was holding back, a finger settled between her collarbones. "This is lovely."

"Thanks. It's from my dad."

He smiled, but didn't move his finger. The one searing its print onto her skin. "I'm really looking forward to seeing your folks this weekend. Your dad has always been one of my idols."

"Yeah, me too." She had a brief flash of what her father would think about her getting so distracted from her task. She'd never seen him prouder of her than when she told him about taking the job with Connor. He was devastated she was moving away, of course, but in his eyes she saw nothing but excitement and love. He believed in her, always.

Connor's hand moved slowly up to her chin. She clenched her fists to keep from trembling. This was as intimate as they'd ever been and she wondered what had changed. Why was he looking at her as though he was seeing something completely different than what he'd always seen?

"I can't thank you enough for today. I know it's above and beyond your job description and I want you to know that I'm grateful. I hope one day I can repay all you've done for me."

How easy it would have been to touch her lips to his, even for the briefest second. How naturally the truth could have come from her mouth. And how impossible both of those were for her. "Let's do this," was the closest she could come.

He gave her a small nod before turning toward the door. The calls of "Mayor Barrett!" erupted as soon as the car doors opened. She tried to make a beeline for the mall entrance but Connor's arm gripped her shoulders and held her in place. Oh, right. They were posing.

This event might have been a fashion intervention for Connor, but she doubted he'd spent even close to the amount of time in preparation as she had. Thankfully, her media-savvy brother had taught her how to stand, how to smile, and how to be consistently photo-ready. She blinked slowly, then opened her eyes wide while tipping her chin down. Just like Jackson had taught her. A slight shift of her head kept her moving from one camera to the next.

They were greeted with applause as soon as they stepped inside the mall. They loved Connor in this part of town. She could imagine that rousing greeting going viral. Proving to everyone that Connor was Virginia's candidate.

Their first stop was John Varvatos, an exclusive men's designer, not only because it was one of Jenna's favorites, but also because they were one of the few stores who agreed to restrict access during their visit. The thought of Connor in one of those suits nearly had her tripping over her own two feet. Hopefully, her nerves would keep her from actually swooning.

The most perfectly-groomed man she'd ever seen greeted them as they entered the store. Even more metrosexual than her brother, which was saying something. She definitely didn't want Connor to go that far - not that he would. His body and temperament would be more aligned to a classic look. With a bit of edge, of course.

Jenna found her groove almost immediately. What she

hadn't told anyone was that going suit shopping had been one of her favorite activities with her dad. He'd given each of his children a special day every month and somehow, picking out his suits became hers. Especially odd since she was the only girl among three brothers.

Connor tried on eight suits on his first trip into the fitting room. Almost every single one looked amazing, but he chose the top six. He wasn't one of those 'let me think about it for an hour' kind of shoppers, thankfully, so they got to final choices with a quick yes or no.

Jenna couldn't tell if he noticed the reactions from the small crowd as he stood in front of the mirrors wearing clothes that fit his lean, muscular build. The dark hair and glasses, paired with a fine dark suit, cut a breathtaking sight.

Through the jokes, the huge number of clothes tried on, even the inseam measurements, he stayed cool as a cucumber. By the third suit, more than a dozen people were weighing in on his choices and he loved it. Inappropriate as it was, Jenna couldn't tear her eyes away as he smiled at the salespeople, ribbed the tailor, and bantered with the media. She loved watching him goof around, make fun of himself, and get even sexier by the second.

A dozen dress shirts, two belts, and several pairs of shoes, chosen with alacrity, were added on to the pile. The bill nearly totaled Jenna's previous year's salary as a schoolteacher.

The staff waved them off as they left the store and Jenna felt as if she'd made a room full of friends. "Wow, that was almost fun."

"Almost?" His eyes glimmered.

"Okay. Actual fun." She looked up at him as they sauntered along the crowded mall walkway, camera crews circling. With her insane heels, the distance to his eyes had been significantly shortened. "You did great. I should have known you were a total ham."

He stopped in front of a department store and took her hand. "Couldn't have done it without you."

"What are you buying next?" a photographer screamed, pulling her out of that delicious moment.

"Actually, we're picking up a few things for Ms. King in here. For any of you who need to leave, I really appreciate your showing up on such short notice. This was a spectacular day!"

Jenna looked around, confused. She wasn't planning on doing any shopping. But maybe he was signaling to all the crews that they could leave. She'd expected that some of them would turn to go, but no one budged.

"Would you mind if we got some more reel of you two shopping?"

Connor tipped his head toward her.

Oh. "Uh... sure."

The clicking began again and Jenna smiled. This whole celebrity thing was turning out to be not so bad at all.

She walked quickly to follow his long strides. "What are we doing here?"

He stopped. "I'm replacing your mascara."

Her brain short-circuited. Her mascara? Much too slowly, it dawned on her. That morning. That awful morning, she'd dropped her mascara in the toilet.

"How did you know?"

"I saw it. In the bathroom. And I described it to Ramona, who told me what it was. They sell that brand here."

Jenna left the department store with four replacements for her ridiculously exorbitant mascara, as well as several small bags filled with products the excited saleswomen had picked out. It might have been enough to make her self-conscious about the attention or the amount of money Connor spent on her, but all she could see was the look of utter happiness on his face.

They spent the rest of the afternoon strolling the length of the mall, stopping for selfies with fans and impromptu conversations about everything from sales tax to healthcare. Connor never got stumped. Not even once. Watching him effortlessly steer conversations, manage the crowds, and dazzle everyone around him made several things clear:

1. Connor Barrett was a rockstar. And her friend.

2. He was so much more layered and interesting than she could have ever imagined.

3. There's nothing she wouldn't do to make sure he achieved his dreams.

CHAPTER 13

*J*enna was all over the internet. Not just her name, but those mile long legs, those graceful arms and the smile that could light up a room. Dread coursed through him, but he just couldn't stop looking, his finger clicking from one site to the next.

Almost unanimously, the internet loved her. Even the sites that would have preferred he and his family disappear from the planet LOVED her. They were calling her Barrett's Babe, the wannabe Senator's starlet, his secret weapon.

Everyone wanted to know their relationship status—some claiming they already did—but they'd dug up everything there was to know about Jenna King. Her educational pedigree, her family's success, her work as a school teacher. They mentioned her Congressman uncle, her tech titan father, and her celebrity brother. One site had titled its story *Bringing California Sunshine to Virginia*. How they'd gotten all that information so fast was beyond him. If only the government worked so efficiently...

Glamorous pictures of her from some gala were interspersed with her as a sweet-faced teenager. Mostly, there were photos and videos from the shopping trip. Her laughing, her blowing air kisses, her holding up shirts for him to try on.

He remembered how nervous she'd been—the first time he'd ever seen her that way. But she'd gone from bothered to beaming within minutes. Still, she hadn't asked for all this exposure and if she was angry, it was his fault. The sites were saying nice things, but she might not have wanted any of it.

He had no idea whether to call her and explain, or hope she wouldn't have seen all of it. At least not before Uncle Robert's party in a few hours. They'd made so much progress since the fiasco at the hotel—she'd even let him hold her hand —he couldn't bear another rift.

His anxiety bubbled to the surface. He needed to do something before it escalated. There was just enough time for some quick calisthenics. Fuck. A hundred pushups might not be enough.

He kept noticing Alex's eyes in the rearview mirror as they navigated the crowded streets of downtown DC. Maybe his bowtie wasn't tied right?

"Hey, Alex. Is something wrong?"

Embarrassment crossed the old man's face. "I'm sorry, sir. I didn't mean to stare. You look very nice."

There was clearly more. "What's wrong, Alex? You can tell me."

"I just wonder about Ms. King. Why we aren't picking her up."

Good question. Except the answer would have to include how he'd royally messed up, driving her into another man's arms, which left him having to take a woman he was never really interested in. "She's actually going with someone else, Alex."

The older man slowly nodded. "I'm sorry about that, sir."

Of course, Alex knew everything. Obi Wan was spot on.

Connor was still thinking about Jenna and Gabe, Jenna and the internet, Jenna and her too smart, too beautiful self, when they pulled into Eleanor's driveway. She was not a suitable match. Wonderful woman with a resume that would impress anyone. She even had all the physical characteristics he'd asked for: a soft, curvy brunette who was the right age and the right everything but completely wrong. All he could think of was a tall, thin blonde built like an athlete with a tiny diamond piercing her left nostril.

Most likely, Gabe was going to sweep her off her feet, if he hadn't already. It hadn't come up—in fact he avoided any mention of the two of them—but he could imagine them together. They were both hip and cool and everything he wasn't. As if having to watch them together wasn't going to be bad enough, Connor would have no time to explain all the photos from today, as he'd have to attend to his own date. Tonight was going to suck.

AUNT OLIVIA GLIDED across the wide room as he entered. "Darling! You're here." She kissed both his cheeks. "I loved all the press on the shopping trip today. You are winning over Virginia, my boy."

"Thank you. Aunt Olivia, this is Eleanor Cullin. Eleanor, Olivia Winston."

The two women air-kissed.

"Lovely to meet you, darlin'," Olivia said, shamelessly examining the woman, head to toe.

Eleanor's face contracted. "And you."

"Where's my dear niece? Didn't you come together?"

Connor held back a grin. Aunt Olivia did not give a rat's

ass about subtlety. Which was made more powerful because it was always covered in so much southern grace and gentility that it was almost impossible to know that her silken words were laced with insults. She'd made her opinion known about Connor's match-made dates, and her clear preference for the newest blonde in his life.

"No, she's coming with Gabe. But you knew that." He matched her smile.

"Oh, who can keep up with you young people? In any case, Uncle Robert is over at the bar. He'd love to see you."

She bowed her head and continued walking toward the next arriving guests.

No sign of Uncle Robert, but Ramona and Lucas were at the bar. Connor had initially found the idea of a black tie birthday party ridiculously ostentatious, but he had to admit, it was a treat to see everyone so dressed up. His best friend, who was stupid good-looking in any situation, looked like a million bucks in a tux. Even his sister, baby bump having grown to baby mound, looked beautiful.

"Hey, you guys."

Lucas went in for a bro-hug. "Con. Looking good, man. The tux is working for you."

"Thanks. You too." He kissed his sister. "Mo, you look beautiful. I didn't know they made dresses like that... for... you know..."

She sighed. "Oh, one shopping trip and now you're a fashion expert. Yes, they make formal maternity gowns. And yes, they are an abomination. Unfortunately, my father-in-law-to-be wasn't so keen on moving the date of his birthday until I give birth to Winnie."

"Winnie?" squeaked Eleanor. "Like Winnie the Pooh?"

Connor caught himself. "Sorry. This is Eleanor. This is my sister, Ramona, and her fiancé, Lucas."

Ramona took her hand. "Nice to meet you. It's just a nickname for the baby. Winnie for Winston. Not for Pooh."

Eleanor offered a flat-lipped smile, either confused or not amused.

Lucas pulled Ramona into his side. "I think you are the most beautiful woman in this room."

She answered with a kiss. Connor wondered how long this phase of constant PDA was going to last.

He glanced around them. "Where's Uncle Robert? And... everyone else?"

Ramona sipped her sparkling water. "Uncle Robert and Uncle Jonathan are having some secret meeting in the kitchen. Might even have to do with your campaign. Aunt Elena is talking to some guy in the band. And-"

A squeal from Olivia cut Ramona off and sent them all spinning toward the entrance. Jackson and Camille had just arrived, looking like something off of a red carpet. Hell, they'd probably been on several of them. Something gleamed behind them and Connor's heart nearly stopped beating.

There she was, sheathed in liquid gold, glowing as if spotlights were following her into the room. Holy fuck. Her dress was simple. None of that sparkly stuff all the other women were wearing. Just a single piece of silky fabric that skimmed over her like water. And the sexiest fucking thing he'd ever seen.

There was no question how perfectly proportioned she was. A smooth curve ran from her shoulders to her waist to her hips. Tits that appeared to be standing up by themselves and legs for days. Red lips, currently spread into a nearly blinding smile.

He blinked as if it was a mirage. She stopped to hug her

aunt, and the tuxedo-clad man with his arm behind her came into view. Everything in his body tensed at the sight of Gabe that close to her. Touching her. Not even the slap of Lucas' hand on his back could make him turn away.

"Hey, Con. You doing all right?"

His best friend's words floated above him as if spoken by a ghost. It didn't matter that everyone could see his stunned expression and probably could decipher why. There was no hiding what was happening in his body or his heart.

Lucas shook him. "Con. Let me know you're okay."

He closed his eyes and dropped his head. "Yeah. I'm fine."

Then an enormous hand was around his arm, pulling him off toward the bathrooms. He twisted free. "What the hell are you doing?"

Lucas met him eye-to-eye. In the decades of their friendship, they'd stood off like this several times. Unfortunately, Lucas had witnessed too many of his episodes, when he'd gone spiraling and needed to be physically restrained. His much larger friend had even sat on him once after he'd flown into a rage at his grandfather's house.

"Con, I understand what's happening here and I want to make sure you've got it handled."

Handled. It's what Jenna always said when he asked for the impossible. He gave his head a brisk shake. "Yeah, sorry. That was rough, watching her..."

"Shit, man. We don't pick the easy ones, huh?"

Lucas' journey to wooing Ramona had been about as bumpy as anything Connor had seen. With Jenna, it wasn't hard. It was impossible. "No." A dejected sigh fell out of him. "You're right. I need to handle it."

"We're here for you. Don't forget that."

Connor stared at his oldest friend who was more like a brother. They'd been to hell and back together. And he'd been such an ass about Lucas' relationship with Ramona. "Sorry," he said for nothing and everything.

They slowly walked back to the bar. His sister's eyes were dark with worry. "You wanna go for a walk, Con?"

She was also familiar with his anxiety, but she was the last one he wanted to worry about him. That little critter in her belly, his niece or nephew, needed to be protected. He kissed her forehead. "Thanks, sis. Maybe later. I still need to find Uncle Robert to wish him a happy birthday."

He put out his hand for Eleanor, who hesitated before taking it. If he could have driven her home right then, he would have. More witnesses to his inevitable breakdown weren't going to be necessary. "Let me introduce you to the rest of the family."

By the time cocktail hour had come to a close and the band was rocking, Connor was almost feeling himself again. Half of Congress had been invited and it was great to have some time with them. Everyone was unequivocally supportive, the work of his very influential mentor, Uncle Robert.

He and Jenna had greeted each other cordially enough, but she was keeping her distance from him. He was sure of it. Which left him staring from a distance. Every glance at her and her date—eating together, dancing, clinking their glasses —set him back a few steps, but he brought himself back on track. Mostly.

That had been the formula for his recovery: fierce determination and a set of prescribed actions that would take down the sensory overload. He'd gotten so good at it that hardly anyone knew. Well, anyone who hadn't known him since childhood. He wasn't sure if Jenna knew, although he could guess that her aunt and uncle might have given her the lowdown.

The birthday boy was currently spinning her around the dance floor, both of them in near hysterics as they attempted a tango. Of course, she was ridiculously graceful. Moved like someone who knew what to do with her body. She was probably a wildcat in bed, all strong limbs, tiny waist, great ass-

What the fuck, Connor? The heat rose simultaneously in his pants and up his throat. He closed his eyes while tapping his foot to pace his breaths. All the sounds of the party faded into the background, his concentration cooling him down.

This had to stop. He was acting like a lovestruck schoolboy with no control over his reactions. He looked up as she planted a dramatic red-lipped kiss on her uncle's cheek.

Or maybe he could man up and stop playing nice.

CHAPTER 14

*C*onnor looked terrible. Well, Connor looked amazing. Like a man in a tuxedo should look. Broad shoulders, lean hips, and a face that set panties on fire. But his expression was nothing but pain. He'd put on a smile when they greeted each other, but she knew it was fake. All those months together had taught Jenna the complete decoding system for Connor Barrett. Something was bothering him and she prayed it wasn't her.

Every time she wanted to sneak away to talk to him, someone else was demanding his attention. With every passing minute, he seemed to be suffering more and more. She looked over at Gabe, chatting up a Congressman, maybe even pimping for some speechwriting work, and wondered if that's what was hurting him. She didn't want to believe it was jealousy. If not, then what?

They'd had such a great day. Perfect, really. And she couldn't believe all the love she was getting on social media. As if she was the celebrity du jour. None of her sketchy past had made an appearance. It was a miracle, and all because of him. But now he looked like he might keel over or punch someone in the face.

"How's my sunshine?" Her father's large hand rested on her back.

She fell into his chest for a hug. "I'm so glad you guys came out for this. It's great to see you."

He pulled her away and crinkled his brow. "Your mother might have come here for the party, but we all know why I'm here." He patted the tip of her nose. "I can't believe how you've transformed, sweetheart. In just a few months, you've blossomed into an even more amazing and powerful woman. I hope you know how proud I am of you. All the guys on the links are so tired of hearing me talk about you, but I don't care."

She beamed back at him. "Oh, Daddy. Thank you, but we haven't even made it through primaries yet."

"You don't worry yourself about that, sunshine. He's all set."

Her smile dropped away. She'd been spying lots of high power conversations that night. Were they about Connor? "How could you know that, Dad? He might have a slight boost this minute, but things change quickly. It's definitely not a done deal."

He shook his head, brown eyes twinkling. "Look around this room, Jenna. Most of the people here are actually running this country. The wheels are already turning for Connor. As long as the two of you keep managing the campaign as you have been, everything will work out."

Jenna had learned some things about her father over the years. She wasn't naive enough to believe that one of the titans of Silicon Valley hadn't had to do some unsavory things to get there. But the statement he'd just made about turning the wheels was one of the scariest things she'd ever heard.

"I don't like the sound of that at all, Dad. It sounds like something *undemocratic* is happening."

He brushed her cheek. "Not at all, sweetheart. We're just making sure that all Robert's colleagues are sending the right message to their constituents."

That hardly sounded better. She caught a glimpse of dark hair across the room. She needed to talk to Connor right away. "Okay, I'm going to go. But I'll see you later." She gave her father a quick kiss before heading toward the bar.

The large group, including Jackson, Camille, Ramona, Lucas, Connor, and his date, were engaged in a rousing discussion. Nobody noticed her so she waited for a break in their conversation. Maybe he already knew what was going on and that's what was upsetting him. In which case, her bringing it up again wasn't going to make him feel better. Maybe she should leave it alone.

"Hey, sis! What are you drinking?" Jackson called.

Connor's expression went from laughing to filled with tension, as it had been every other time she'd seen him that night. Maybe he was mad at her. "Uh... nothing right now, thanks. I just need to borrow Connor for a second."

It seemed like everyone had an opinion about that, from the looks on their faces, not least of which was his date, who openly scowled. It took Connor a beat to break out of the clump and step toward her.

"Hey. What's up?"

There was nothing good about the way he said that. As if he was trying to sound casual while dying.

"Can you come with me for a second?"

He turned back to the group. "I'll be right back."

Since when had she become the outsider? She didn't like it one bit.

She led him to an empty spot in the middle of the room. "I

wanted to let you know about something I just heard. My father-"

"Mustn't stand on the dance floor," Aunt Olivia said while breezing by them in a spin. "It's for dancing!"

Without hesitation, he took her hand and put his arm around her. Jenna followed with a palm on his shoulder. Everything felt hot, especially his hand on her low back and his breath on her neck. Shit. It was going to be very hard to hold a thought standing this close to him. God, it felt good to be in his arms.

He brought his mouth to her ear, his lips brushing against her cheek. "You look stunning tonight, Jenna. If you haven't heard that enough."

Not from you. "Thanks. You, too. You can really carry a tux."

He pulled her in as he quickened his steps. She followed, his solid chest pressed against hers. As they slowed, she slid her hand around his neck. In one move, she could be kissing his neck, along his jaw, breathing in his clean, fresh scent, tasting his skin.

"You wanted to tell me something?"

It was as if she'd just crash landed back on Earth. "Oh, right. My dad said a really funny thing to me. He said that Uncle Robert and all his Congresspeople friends were turning the wheels for you. I don't know... it just sounded... illicit to me."

"I see."

She waited for him to continue, but he just kept dancing. She separated their bodies to look at him. "Aren't you worried? Or upset?"

He shook his head. "No. I don't think it means anything as dramatic as you imagine. They're just making sure their people know they're backing my candidacy. There won't be any vote rigging or tampering, if that's what you think."

He was brushing this off much too easily. "You don't seem fazed by this at all."

"I'm not. It's how this country is run. For better or worse."

He pulled her back in and she didn't resist. It felt like a curtain had been lifted, revealing a great big steaming pile of shit. And if that wasn't what was upsetting him, what was it?

"Is everything all right?" she asked.

She noticed the stutter in his otherwise smooth steps.

"Fine. Why do you ask?"

"You've looked upset all night. I wasn't sure if you were mad... or something."

He tipped her body back in a small dip. "Nope. Are you mad about anything?"

What would she be mad about? "No. I thought today was amazing. More fun than I've had in a long time."

The song ended, but he didn't stop swaying. Which was perfectly fine with her. She had no interest in peeling her body off his.

"That's good to hear. I felt the same way."

As the rising lilt of a violin filled the silence, her other hand slid behind his neck. His palm pressed into her low back while the other landed between her shoulders. She couldn't tell whose heart was beating so hard that she could almost hear it. He brushed his cheek across her temple, which felt like the recognizable beginning of a kiss. She pressed in, the line of his jaw on a trajectory to her mouth. She gripped his neck, waiting for-

"May I?"

At first she though he was asking, but that wasn't his voice. She opened her eyes to see Gabe standing directly in front of her. How long had he been there? Shit.

It felt like forever until Connor released his grip enough that she could separate from him. Not that she wanted to.

Gabe quirked his eyebrow. "I'd love to have this dance with my gorgeous date."

Connor's torso expanded with a slow, deep breath. Still holding her body, he nodded at Gabe. "Of course."

She slid from one man to another, trying to hide crushing disappointment. If Gabe hadn't shown up, would Connor really have kissed her, right there in the middle of the party? It felt like it. But it couldn't be. Maybe all the pressure was getting to him and he was losing his bearings. Since that terrible morning at the hotel, all of his reliable control seemed to be dissolving. She'd heard all about his issues as a teenager and hoped he wasn't slipping into some dangerous pattern. Even the Senate wasn't worth him losing himself.

"Having fun, JK?"

Her attention snapped back to the man whose arms were currently carrying her across the dance floor. She wasn't sure when she'd have to let Gabe down, but it was imminent. There was absolutely nothing wrong with him. Except, of course, that he wasn't Connor.

"Yes, thanks."

The rest of the evening passed with no more almost-kisses. At least Connor's pained expression had disappeared after their dance. Maybe he needed reassurance of her commitment to him, that she wouldn't get distracted from their single focus. She wasn't sure how much clearer she could be that he was her top priority. The whole guy thing wasn't going to be solved that night, but at least she knew they were okay. Or hoped they were.

SHE ARRIVED at her empty house, after declining Gabe many,

many times. God, that man was persistent. Thankfully, there was no question what her answer would be. Any attraction she might have had for him dissolved during that dance with Connor.

As soon as she got into bed, all the regret flooded in. She should have gone to the party with Connor. She shouldn't have reacted so badly in the hotel. Camille's view of the situation was making more and more sense. If there was still a campaign after the primaries in two days, she was going to consider the possibility of something other than a professional relationship. She was going to be brave.

CHAPTER 15

*J*enna came skipping out of her house before the car had come to a stop in the driveway. Even before Connor could get out and greet her at the door, which would've been the gentlemanly thing to do. Dragging her out on a Sunday morning was bad enough. Acting like it was no big deal would be unforgivable.

Over the past two days, he'd seen her at work, where she looked like the boss, on their shopping trip, where she looked like a star, and at the party, where that nearly-there slip of silk nearly broke him. But that morning, in her simple, flowery dress, she looked comfortable, happy and like someone he'd never get tired of being around. It crossed his mind that if he lost the race, he wouldn't be starting every morning seeing her. His chest clenched at the thought.

She slipped into the car. "Hey, good morning, guys!"

"Good morning, Ms. King. Lovely, as always, to see you."

She squeezed Alex's shoulder. "Thank you, Alex. So sorry for dragging you out on such a beautiful Sunday. Maggie must be cursing us."

"Not at all, Ms. King. I'm telling you, she's never going to let me retire. Whenever I'm home for more than a few hours, she's pushing me out the door. And, you know how grateful I am to be involved in what you wonderful people are up to."

"Oh, Alex. You're the wonderful one. I don't know what we would do without you."

"I do appreciate you saying that, Ms. King."

Connor watched, mesmerized. Every time he thought he'd figure her out, she'd pull out some other magic trick. Except, they weren't tricks. It was as if she was letting more and more of her true personality out and he couldn't get enough.

Nearly everyone else who'd been in the car with Alex had either treated him like a servant or disregarded him entirely. The way she made the people around her feel seen and appreciated was awe-inspiring. It might have been the single most important factor in the success of his team. And the reason they all, Alex included, would do anything for her.

She sat back in her seat. "How are you feeling this morning, Connor?"

He'd been up since dawn, working out and doing his breathing exercises, contemplating his next steps. Their moment at the party made it clear—he needed to up his game if he was going to have a shot. It would have to be done appropriately, of course. He'd learned his lesson at the hotel.

"Great. Had a killer workout and am ready for some pancakes." His invitation to christen a new restaurant in town was going to have a fluffy, delicious perk that morning.

"Pancakes, really?" She flashed that megawatt smile. "How decadent of you."

She had no idea how decadent he could be. "I think I deserve it. Don't you?"

Her eyes twinkled with mischief. "Of course you do. And

I'm pleased you've chosen pancakes instead of anything more... hedonistic."

"Nice word, King. Nice word."

He joined her, leaning against the upholstered seat-back, but not before slipping his hand over hers. When she curled her fingers around his, he knew it was going to be a great day.

THEY RETURNED to the car with full bellies and smiling faces. It had gone even better than expected.

"Okay, Alex, there were too many delicious options to choose from so I got you my two favorites. You can share with Maggie. Or have it all yourself, of course."

There she went again. He hadn't even seen her order those two extra meals. Her thoughtfulness had been directed at Alex, but Connor felt like he was the luckiest one in that car.

Their only other appointment for the day was a financial meeting with Ramona. She'd been managing all of the campaign's money in the background. His sister strongly disliked the world of politics, to put it mildly, but she could raise money better than anyone on the planet. Her pregnancy and her distaste kept her shielded from the day-to-day, but she'd somehow managed to keep the campaign constantly flush.

Connor dropped his eyes as they passed his old family home, which had been sitting empty since his father had died six months earlier. Neither he nor Ramona could get themselves to sell it. Everything was still too raw and painful. They'd have to do something, eventually, but for now, it just sat, sad and bare. He made a mental note to talk to his sister about it. After the primaries.

They arrived at her house, which used to be Lucas' house.

All those years back, when Lucas ditched his bachelor pad and bought a family house in the suburbs, Connor couldn't have imagined that the family would include Lucas, Ramona, and their baby. Wild.

Connor walked right in without knocking, an unbreakable habit after years of full access. Ramona appeared out of the kitchen wearing what must have been one of Lucas' t-shirts and a pair of basketball shorts.

She squeezed his arm while giving Jenna a kiss. "Good thing I wasn't walking around naked, Con."

"Don't be gross, Mo. Nobody wants to see all that."

Jenna punched him in the arm. Hard. "Don't be rude, Connor. Your sister is gorgeous. I can only hope I look half as good when I'm pregnant."

Any pain he might have felt in his arm combusted in the brain explosion of Jenna's statement. He had a million questions about the whole *when I'm pregnant* idea, but now was not the time to ask.

"Come in the kitchen. I'm making fuh."

He followed along, but had no idea what the hell his sister had just said.

"Oh, my God, I love fuh!" Jenna said. "Have you been to that place near Columbia Circle? Their bubble tea is amazing, too."

"Yeah, it's great. But ever since Lucas taught me how to make it, I just have it at home. It's one of the few things that Winnie doesn't try to evict."

The first several months of Ramona's pregnancy had nearly killed her. She was throwing up all day long. Even had to be hospitalized. Of course, their father's death didn't help. Thank God she was doing better.

He raised his hand. "I have questions."

Ramona rolled her eyes. "Yes, Connor."

"What the hell are you two talking about? And when did you learn how to cook?"

She glared at him. "We're talking about fuh. You know, P H O. The Vietnamese noodle soup. And I haven't learned to cook. I just follow my brilliant fiancé's clear and simple instructions. He preps the broth and all the veggies and I assemble."

"Okay, that makes more sense." Nobody would ever accuse his sister of domesticity. At least not before she'd moved back to Virginia.

"You should try it. I'll make you a bowl."

"Cool."

Jenna spun her head around, big blue eyes swallowing him whole. "What? Aren't you stuffed? You just ate about a hundred pancakes."

He rubbed his belly. "No. I'm good. Some noodle soup sounds awesome." He peered into the large pot on the stove. "It's spicy, right?"

"No. But I'll get you some hot sauce." Ramona looked over her shoulder. "Can I get you some, Jenna?"

She shook her head in disbelief. "No thanks, Ramona. I couldn't fit another thing in my body. I can't believe Connor is eating again after the breakfast we had."

Ramona sprinkled some green stuff on top of the steaming bowl. "My brother is a furnace. You must have noticed that. Couldn't hold on to body-fat to save his life. Fucker."

Ramona walked the bowl over to the large wooden table and went back to assemble a second one. "It looks like you are two, Miss Skinny Pants. The two of you are like bean-poles."

There was absolutely nothing that resembled a bean-pole on Jenna's body. Unless beanpoles now had broad shoulders, amazing tits, and a peach of an ass. He headed toward the table and sat down before the situation in his pants became public.

"THAT WAS GREAT," Connor said after the last spoonful of soup. "Maybe you can take me to that place you were talking about."

Jenna nodded, taking a sip of iced ginger tea, the other one of Ramona's pregnancy staples. "Yeah. Definitely."

Ramona patted her belly, which was surprisingly heartwarming. He had to admit it took him a while to get on the baby train. He would never have guessed his sister would want a husband and family. The entirety of her life had been spent running from any hints of that. She was as confirmed a single woman as he'd ever known. Love changed everything for her. Love with the right guy.

"So, you're in great shape, financially. We'll have to revisit after the primaries, but I have a detailed plan for increasing our coffers ten-fold. There are a few big guns holding out to see how you do."

He stood up and kissed his sister on the top of her head. "Have I mentioned you're the best?"

"No. You did call me gross, though."

"Sorry, Mo. You know what an ass I can be."

She and Jenna shared a laugh. "Trust me, I know. And I'm glad to see those days are mostly over."

Jenna looked at Ramona as if something dawned on her. Her whole body softened in a way he'd seen after she solved a tough problem. The question remained—was he the problem or the solution?

CONNOR STEPPED into his house and instead of relief, encountered a grip of emptiness. He'd been looking forward to a quiet night, one of the rare few with no meetings, dinners, or events of any kind. Over the past several months, he could count on one hand the number of times he'd been idle. The campaign schedule had been grueling and he loved it. But that night, with his sister resting, his best friend working, and Jenna spending time with her parents, he found himself pacing alone in his living room. Being inactive was not his friend.

It had been a good day. The last minute decision to take Jenna to his father's house had been hard, emotionally, but he was glad he got to share that with her. His dad would have absolutely loved her—so smart, funny, and beautiful, with a wild streak and unrelenting kindness. He could have imagined them hanging out, telling dumb jokes, and making fun of the DC stiffs. Maybe he would have painted a lovely portrait of her.

Connor swallowed a lump of sadness. Being busy had helped with the grief, but seeing that house again brought all those buried emotions forward. His father was dead.

That thought halted his steps and hitched his breath. All the emotional frenzy of the past week descended on him like a building. Hiding his feelings about Jenna... the huge ups and downs of the campaign... the growing distance between him and his goal... all heavy and suffocating.

His heart beat like an alarm. *Get a hold of yourself, Connor.* Things could go badly if he let this escalate.

He needed to see her. If she was there, with him, he'd be able to breathe better. He picked up his phone, then put it down. He needed to give her space, let her have a night to herself. She deserved time away from the relentless strain of the campaign and all of his craziness. Maybe he'd head over to Winston's and see Lucas.

The more he thought about that idea, walked it out, the better it sounded. He'd get out of the house, see his friend, maybe even hang with some fans. Everyone knew that the restaurant was a safe zone for politicians so he was unlikely to get swarmed. Yes, that was a great idea. And it wouldn't hurt to extend Jenna an invitation. He blew a breath from his pursed lips as he picked up the phone one more time.

Connor used the staff entrance to Winston's and made his way through the bustling kitchen. He could have probably gone in the front, but he'd gotten used to the back entrance. Lucas looked up as he tossed something in a sizzling pan. Hopefully, he'd be able to duck out and say hello when things quieted down.

The bar was nearly empty, surprising in contrast to the busy dining room. Connor picked a stool with a good view of the large front door. He smoothed down the front of his light blue shirt, the one he chose because it matched his favorite eyes. Jenna would be arriving any minute now.

CHAPTER 16

*J*enna saw him, cradling a glass of scotch and smiling, as soon as she entered the restaurant. Connor got to his feet and clamped his gaze on her so fiercely she reached her hand for a wooden railing to steady herself. He was wearing one of the new shirts they'd bought on their shopping trip. An almost imperceptibly light blue, fit close to his sleek frame and unspeakably hot.

Goosebumps sprinkled over her arms as he reached for her and then kissed her on the cheek. This was a new greeting.

"Thanks for coming."

She laid her hand on the bar and sat on the padded leather stool, grateful for the coolness of the surfaces. "Sure. My folks called it a night pretty early. Their flight leaves first thing in the morning, so I was just at home."

"Well, you're a great sport." He adjusted his glasses. "Always."

If he only knew that she'd been sitting at home, scrolling through the TV channels, trying desperately not to think about him. And failing. "You act like it's such an imposition.

It's not like you asked me to go dig up dead bodies or something."

He flinched.

Maybe that was too much. Especially after they'd been to his recently-deceased father's house. She bit her lip.

"Negroni for you?"

Perfect. Her favorite cocktail. "Yes, thanks."

They sat in silence for the first few sips of her drink. Something about him made her question whether he was at ease or not.

She touched his arm. "How are you holding up?"

He turned to face her a bit too quickly. "Fine. Good. Why do you ask?"

"Well, it's a tense time. I would imagine that the stress is through the roof."

The line of his lips flattened. "Yeah. But it's important I manage it. So I do."

She nodded, unsure of what to say. She wasn't expecting it would feel so awkward to be hanging out with him, socially. It had never been like that before, but maybe that's because they always had plenty of work to discuss. She swirled her drink and took another sip.

"How was dinner?"

She smiled. Dinner with her parents, Jackson, and Camille had been a blast. She'd wanted so badly to invite him, but thought it would be inappropriate. And would lead to a whole slew of questions about their *relationship* that she wasn't ready to answer. But he would have loved it. Connor and her father were so similar—formidable men, equal parts ambitious, dorky, and fiercely loyal to their families.

"It was great. And I successfully refrained from grilling my dad about his sketchy remark at the party. It's still bothering me, but I'm trying to let it go."

He stroked her hand. "It's part of the game, Jenna. You might want to prepare yourself for things to get much more... complicated... as the campaign progresses."

That was not particularly good news. Except for the statement about the campaign progressing. She wanted him to feel hopeful. "Okay, I'll try not to act like a wide-eyed ingenue."

"Weeeeeell, look who's heeeere. Connor Barrett!"

The booming, slurring voice approached them, coming from a squat, red-faced man. It wasn't clear if he was drunk or had a drawl.

Connor stood slowly. He was a pro at dealing with the public. "Hi. How are you tonight?"

"Fiiiiine. Just fiiiiine. Surprised to see *you* here, though."

"Winston's is the best place in town. How was your dinner?"

The man curled his lip and looked Jenna up and down. "Better before I saw you."

Oh shit. Jenna had encountered some haters and hecklers—it was inevitable—but this felt imminently dangerous.

Connor tipped his head. "Sorry to hear that, my friend. I-"

"You ain't my friend, you elitist assssssshole."

Jenna's attention swept to the commotion behind the bar as one of the bartenders rushed out.

Connor put up his hands. "Okay, man. I hear you. I'm not here to disturb you."

"All done with your faggot shopping trip? Showing off how much money you and your family keep stealin' from the people of Virginia? When are the Barrett crooks gonna get the hell outta here? So tired of seein' all your stuck-up faces. Y'all should be in jail!"

Connor stood a full head taller than the angry man, and

she could almost see the heat pouring off his body. Fear brought a quiver to her breath. Fuck.

"Listen, man. I'm not bothering you. Why don't you go back to your party and-"

"Why don't you get the fuck out of here?" The man jutted a finger into Connor's face. "And take your California bitch with you. Whoring around like she owns the place."

It all happened in slow motion—the spit flying out of the man's face, the bend of Connor's elbow, his fist heading toward the man's face, and a blur of white shoving Connor back. She was thrust against the bar as the bartender jumped in front of the man. Shouts and gasps filled the restaurant.

Lucas had his arms wrapped around Connor, pinning him. A sea of phones, recording the incident, pointed toward them. She couldn't catch her breath.

All of a sudden, it was so quiet, she could hear Connor's raspy breaths and Lucas' whispers. Almost as if he was reciting a mantra or hypnotizing him.

"Jenna."

Someone was saying her name.

"Jenna!"

Lucas had one hand on Connor's chest, but was facing her.

She looked from one man to the other. "Yes. What?"

"Take him home." It wasn't a request.

"But I didn't drive. I-"

Lucas hardened his expression. "Take his car and drive him home." Every word enunciated as if she had gone dumb.

She swallowed and nodded. Lucas turned to Connor again, more whispers passing between them, before handing Jenna a key fob. "It's in the back lot. You'll have to go through the restaurant." He looked down and scrubbed a palm across his face. "You know... right?"

Connor's situation, which she'd only ever heard about, was now clear. "Yes. I know."

HER HANDS SHOOK as she plugged his address into her navigation app. He sat nearly motionless in the passenger seat, eyes closed, his foot tapping out an even rhythm. She concentrated on the road and driving the unfamiliar car the short distance to his house.

By the time they arrived, he looked like himself again. Muscles of his face relaxed, breathing back to normal, moving smoothly. He opened his front door and held it as she walked in. She hadn't recovered quite as well, still shaken about what happened at the bar and wondering what she was doing at his house.

Unsure of what he was expecting, she followed him down a hallway and into a room. His bedroom. She turned to walk out.

He took her hand. "Please don't go. I'll be right out."

He walked into what she assumed was the bathroom without an answer. The water ran, followed by a low groan. He must have stepped into a cold shower.

Jenna dropped onto the edge of the bed, body still trembling. Fuck, fuck, fuck.

When he came out, soaking wet, wearing only a towel, the trembling became full blown shock. Everything about what was happening shouldn't be. He opened a drawer, pulled out shorts, dropped his towel, and put them on. Maybe she registered the sensations that his naked body, shadowed in the dimly lit room, elicited in her own body, but it never made it as far as her conscious mind. Every part of her skin burned.

"Lie down with me. Please."

As if she was now the one under hypnosis, she pulled off

her shoes and scooted toward the headboard. She lay back, fully dressed, body stiff with tension, desire, and a swirl of shock that left her dazed.

He crawled onto the bed and curled his long body into her, laying his head on her chest, his wet hair soaking the top of her dress. She wrapped an arm around him, his skin cold to the touch, and drew her hand across his hair.

"I'm sorry, Jenna. So sorry."

At that moment, she realized three things about her situation:

1. Nothing would be the same between them after that night.

2. This was not a man whose emotions she could toy with.

3. She was falling for Connor Barrett.

"It's okay. I've got you." She held him, and stroked his head, until his body relaxed into sleep.

She woke with a start, still flat on her back, in an otherwise empty bed. She ran her tongue across her grimy teeth. Ugh. A quick trip to the bathroom and a rinse with the purple mouthwash in the cabinet didn't help her feel any more normal. Or less awkward.

She followed the sound of his voice all the way into the kitchen on the other side of the house. He was pacing, phone against his hear, nodding. He handed her a mug of coffee. "Yeah, yeah. Got it. That's fine. Jenna and I are here, we can hash out a plan. No, it's fine. Gabe doesn't have to-" He took a sip from his own mug. "Right. Okay, yeah. I guess so. Later."

He put the phone down and took another sip. He looked at her, but said nothing.

Her cheeks warmed. "Good morning."

He slipped his fingers under his glasses and rubbed his

eyes. "I hardly know what to say to you, Jenna. At some point, you deserve a full explanation, and an apology, and-"

She put up a hand. "It's okay. You don't owe me anything."

He laughed. "The extent of what I owe you cannot be overstated. But right now, we've got a huge amount of damage control to do. The team is on their way over."

She looked down at her crumpled clothes. "Oh. Okay."

He took two steps toward her and stopped, inches away. Then his arms reached around and pulled her in. "One day, I hope you'll be able to think of me as more than the man who..." He squeezed tighter. So tight, it almost hurt. "I'm more than that man."

JENNA TRIED to ignore the odd looks from Luisa, Daniel, and especially Gabe as they sat around Connor's living room. It was obvious she'd spent the night. She was in all the now-viral videos of Connor in his near-fight, wearing the same exact clothes. But their plans for the day were more important than her discomfort.

After they'd figured out how to clean things up with the Virginian people, she'd have to fix the message with team. Regardless of what happened, or would happen, with Connor, she needed her crew to not get distracted or confused by her role. The last thing she wanted was for them to think she was only interested in nailing her boss. Despite how much they respected her, she knew better than to think that she could prevent the normal thought processes that always prosecuted the women in bed with powerful men.

Daniel waved his publicity magic wand. Somehow, he figured out how to spin the whole thing into a chivalrous defense of her honor and an indictment of the false separations that were tearing the country apart. The man in the bar was rebranded as a drunk degenerate, which wasn't so far from the truth. They had already planned a full day of meet-n-greets, so the only change was the content of the message.

By the time Alex arrived to pick her up and take her home, they were all ready to rock it.

"Good morning, Ms. King." Alex smiled as he held the car door open.

"Good morning, Alex. Sorry about the last minute call."

"Oh, Ms. King, I wish you would stop thinking that you are inconveniencing me. I am so happy to be serving you."

They met eyes in the rearview mirror several times. "Thank you, Alex."

"I know you have a big day ahead of you..."

The way he said that communicated something different than his usual statements. "You know what happened."

"Maggie is on all that internet stuff. She showed me."

Yeah, the world was watching. "Pretty rough. But we can handle it."

"I just want you to know, Ms. King, that I've known Mr. Barrett since he was in diapers. One of the best men I've ever known. Sometimes, he gets a little... stressed. But that's because he cares too much. He's an admirable man."

More than admirable. A man to turn your life upside-down for. "I know, Alex. I know."

CHAPTER 17

*I*t had been a crazy combination of the best and the worst night of Connor's life. A lifetime spent trying not to lose control vanished in the face of that animal's insults. Like a repeat of another time. An awful time. But then, she was holding him, his ear against her pounding heart, her whispers penetrating his shame and fear.

While he knew how damaging it had all been, and how hard he would have to work to regain the confidence of the people, he wasn't sure he would undo any of it. Not if it meant he wouldn't have spent the night in her arms.

He entered the middle school auditorium, their first stop of the day, to talk to a gathering of local teachers and parents about educational reform. He hadn't expected this crowd to be up on the previous night's debacle, but he was dead wrong. It came up immediately.

He caught himself wanting to pace across the old wooden floor of the stage and forced his feet to hold still beneath him. Stanley's voice echoed in his head: "Makes you look shifty when you pace like that." This was going to be the first run of the new message and he wanted to get it right. He paused and took off his glasses.

The words did not flow as easily as he would have liked, but he made it clear that he regretted his actions. Then he turned the conversation to the frustrations that arose when people didn't have enough opportunities in their lives. That segued directly to his plan for increasing Virginia's low literacy rate.

He braced himself for a retort, or even more questions, but none came. From that point forward, he pre-empted all the rumors and conjecture by bringing up the event every time he spoke. By the fourth or fifth re-telling, he was even able to infuse some humor into it. He made fun of his reputation as a nerd by pulling off his glasses and standing like Superman. The crowds loved it.

Jenna never wavered, with every stop and every speech and every difficult round of questions. Virginia had fallen in love with her and the mention of someone demeaning her sent the crowds wild. Handmade billboards that read *We Love Our California Girl* filled the rooms. She joined him onstage at their third stop at his, and the crowds' insistence. His message, which had started out as an apology for his outburst, became an indictment of violence against women.

And it just got bigger—more people, more excitement, more support as the day went on. The trolls were still flaming social media, but the people who came out to see him—see *them*—were unanimously in support.

In a nearly flawless day, filled with moments he wouldn't soon forget, there stood pieces of time that left him speechless and breathless. After every stop, they returned to the car, no words needed as they sat back in their seats and she took his hand.

His discomfort crept back in minutes before they arrived

at her house. After a day of quick-thinking and consistent eloquence, he had no fucking idea how to ask Jenna to stay with him. He rehearsed about a hundred different options in his head and nothing sounded right. It had to be in every way different than her involuntary care-taking the night before, but not just a booty call. It wasn't even about sex. Or, at least, not *only* about sex. He wanted to sit with her and hold her hand and share some time together before it all happened tomorrow. Before the voters determined whether his campaign would continue or not.

"Everything all right?" Her eyes were tired but so bright. He could get lost in those eyes.

"Yeah. I can't believe we pulled it off today. I thought I'd be dodging tomatoes." He ran his fingers across her wrist. "As usual, you made it happen. You saved the day."

"I'm just glad you're feeling better."

His heart sank. She was still thinking about the night before. Not what he was hoping, but who could blame her. She'd probably be reliving that night for a long time. Having to hold a grown man while he fought his demons was probably as far from an aphrodisiac as a root canal.

He would have to wait until it wasn't so fresh in her memory. Until he created a new association in her mind about him as a man. A good, strong, capable man. One who didn't get into fights. One who could love her like she deserved to be loved.

"I am. Thanks."

"You did great today." She paused before turning her gaze, all soft and warm, to him. "Get some rest, okay?"

He kept a hold of her hand and tried desperately to hide his resistance. He wanted to keep her there, with him, turn the car around and go back to his house. She wouldn't invite him in—he knew that—propriety was too important to her.

The right words wouldn't come. He'd have to let her go. His grip loosened enough for her to free her hand. "Have a good night, Jenna."

"Thanks, Connor. You too."

He forced a smile, his heart bursting and breaking all at the same time.

⁂

CONNOR WOKE WELL before his five am alarm, itching to get to the gym. Election day had finally arrived and he expected his anxiety to be through the roof. Instead, he pulsed with excitement. The good kind. No matter how the day ended up, he was ready. He'd proven to himself that he had what it takes. And he had a clear plan to get the woman, too. He could have everything he wanted.

He and Lucas sat in the steam room after a double—two hours of their typical Crossfit workout. There were moments he felt like his heart might explode out of his chest, his muscles might catch on fire, and his best friend might never forgive him, but damn did it feel good now that it was done.

Lucas looked him up and down. "You're looking good, man. Ripped. Have you upped your workouts?"

"In a desperate attempt to work off all that sexual frustration. You've seen Jenna, right?"

Lucas made a face. "You mean my *cousin*, Jenna?"

"Hey, I think that's still legal next state over."

Lucas punched him in the arm. "I'm good. With your sister, by the way. The one carrying my child."

Connor put his hands up. "Okay, okay, you win."

"You know I love you, man. And I'm so fucking proud of you."

Connor punched him back. "I know."

"I also need to say, don't worry about what happened with Jenna the other night. She's no delicate daisy. She's strong as hell. And this little thing... well... it's not going to scare her away."

"I wish I was as sure as you. I mean, having a woman cradle you to sleep while you're curled up like a fucking baby isn't a great starting point for a relationship." Even the memory brought a sour taste to Connor's mouth.

"Well, next time—and I'm sure there's going to be a next time—you show her the man who's not cowering."

"It's just so far from normal."

"It's not like you ever did things like normal people anyway, Con."

"Oh, looks who's talking. You waited for Ramona for how long? Fifteen years?"

"That's why we're friends, dude."

"We're not going to be much longer if I have to sit in this steam room for one more minute." Lucas stood up. "I'm out."

THE TWO MEN headed to their respective homes to get ready for the day. Connor had planned the day in detail, starting with visits to his biggest supporters. So many people had put his posters in their windows, gathered their communities for rallies, and publicly defended him, over and over. He'd attracted an extraordinary audience of ordinary citizens standing up for themselves and calling bullshit when they heard it. These were the people he'd been fighting for, and he appreciated them fighting for him.

Connor walked the few blocks from his last visit to the polling place to cast his vote, all his energy adding an extra skip to his step. He had to hold back from outright running. Another three blocks took him to the campaign office, which he hoped would be empty. Some time there, by himself, to absorb everything that had happened that year, would have been therapeutic. It was the end of the road for that part of his life, no matter what happened. They'd be vacating, if he lost, or moving to a bigger space, if he won.

Luisa jumped when he opened the door. "Oh, good morning, Mayor Barrett."

His plans for time alone were dashed. "Luisa, please call me Connor. Seriously."

"No. I'm going to be calling you Senator Barrett soon enough. You'll just have to live with it."

She was an exceptional woman. Worked well with everyone and had been invaluable. He hoped she liked the thank you gift he'd picked out for her.

"Why are you here so early?" he asked.

She slipped a stack of papers into the recycling bin. "I wanted to make sure I was here for the caterers."

He'd ordered breakfast and lunch for the entire staff so they could hang out and watch as the results came in. He put out his hand for her. "Thank you for everything. It's been an honor to work with you."

She dipped her head. "And you, Mayor."

He walked to the back corner of the small space and stood in front of his messy desk. The only place in his life that he allowed to be disorganized. Maybe this would be a good time to finally get it cleaned off. He could give himself a fresh start.

"Finally doing something about that disaster of a desk?"

That voice. His face erupted in a smile he couldn't stop as he slowly turned to see his favorite person. "Hey, there."

Jenna leaned against the doorframe in a beautiful blue dress. The same blue as the Virginia state flag. "I didn't expect to see you for a few more hours."

He gave her a half shrug. "I heard there were going to be pancakes."

She took the few steps to him and rubbed a hand down his arm. "Holding up okay?"

He flinched. He hated the idea of her seeing him as weak or incapable. "I don't want you to worry about me."

She pulled her hand away, which made it even worse. "I'm not worried about you, Connor. I know who you are."

***

THE NEWS STATIONS called it by five pm. One of the most definitive wins in the state's history. The first call he didn't let go to voicemail was from Uncle Robert. Although it was his mentor in his ear, offering him congratulations, it was her eyes he looked into. Her big, blue eyes brimming with tears. They'd done it. Against all odds, they'd won the nomination.

As soon as he hung up the call, he wrapped Jenna in a hug and spun her around. She stumbled as he put her down, grinning like a kid on Christmas morning. He could hardly stand in the beam of her smile.

"Congratulations, candidate. You did it."

"*We* did it. I know exactly who made this happen, and she doesn't have dark hair or glasses."

She shook her head. "Nope. It was you, Connor."

He grabbed her shoulders. "You and I both know that isn't-"

"Anyway... how would you like to celebrate? Would you like me to call Lucas and see if we can get the private room at Winston's? Or someplace new? Anything you want."

He knew exactly what he wanted. He fixed his gaze onto

her bright eyes, not letting go of her shoulders. "Actually, I want to go home, put on an old t-shirt, sit on my couch, and watch bad TV. Maybe even scratch my balls."

She almost looked disappointed, which was unexpected. "That's quite an image."

"Is that okay?" He ran his thumbs across the front of her shoulders, heart beating so loud it created a rush in his ears.

"Yes." She nodded and gave him what looked like a forced smile. "We'll get you home. I don't blame you for wanting to be alone. It's been crazy and you must be exhausted."

The thumb-rubbing stopped and his grip tightened. He cinched his brows in confusion. "I don't want to be alone, Jenna. This plan involves you sitting right next to me."

She let out a big breath and everything brightened. "Hopefully scratching my balls isn't required."

"Purely optional."

CHAPTER 18

*J*enna spent the short ride to Connor's house thrilled and terrified. This was really happening. Not that she knew *what* was happening. But this invitation felt like it meant something.

As expected, a crowd of paparazzi camped out on his front lawn. They all snapped to attention as the Towncar pulled into the driveway. Alex stopped the car. Connor had already done a dozen interviews at the office. She squeezed his arm. God, she loved how it felt to touch him. "Want to talk to these folks?"

He looked out the window at the cameras, perched and ready to capture any movement. "I think I'm done for tonight."

She couldn't blame him. "Good."

Alex continued pulling into the garage. Before he stepped out of the car, Jenna touched his shoulder. "Can you hold on for a sec, Alex?"

"Of course, Ms. King."

She faced Connor. "I'm assuming the house is empty. No

food or drink?" Having seen the inside of his fridge, she already knew the answer.

He squinted. "Yup."

She could take care of that. And maybe a solo trip to the grocery store would give her time to figure out a strategy for the evening. Get mentally prepared. "Okay, I'll handle it." She smiled at his look of surprise. "I don't think you should step one foot outside if you don't want to get swarmed."

"I don't mean to intrude." Alex turned to face them. "I'd be happy to pick up anything you need. I think the two of you deserve a nice, quiet night at home."

Something about the way he said that sent an excited tickle up her spine. His emphasis on *the two of you* pointed to a possibility she could hardly imagine.

Connor put on his happy face. "That's perfect, Alex. Thank you so much." He took her hands, excitement flickering all over those whisky brown eyes. "What should we have?"

Maybe some time apart wouldn't be necessary after all. "You go in, I'll make a list. See you in a minute. Make sure the AC is on. I don't want to cook in there."

She pulled a piece of paper out of her notebook and began scribbling away. Falafel from Shawarma Shack. Connor's favorite beer from the small specialized liquor store the next town over. A long list of staples – eggs, bread, fruit, his favorite cheeses, a large bag of celery, her favorite snack, and of course popcorn for the movie. She handed the list to Alex, and then immediately pulled it out of his hand.

"I can't believe I almost forgot the most important thing. The largest bag you can find of mini Twix. I know they're not healthy for him, but I can't deny him. It's his only vice."

Alex flashed her his sweet smile. "I wish my only vice were tiny candy bars."

"You and me both, Alex."

She reached into her wallet and pulled out a card. "Here, use this. My pin is 0928."

He waved his hand. "I already have the business card for the campaign, Ms. King."

"No, we won't use that. Put it on mine."

He nodded before exiting the car and opening her door.

"Oh, and Alex. Buy yourself whatever you'd like to eat. And maybe a great bottle of wine for you and Maggie. After this, you'll have the rest of the night off. I promise."

The older man gifted her with one of his ultra deep belly laughs that always warmed her heart. "I'll see you shortly. You go on inside and get ready for a wonderful, relaxing night. You deserve it."

Jenna stepped into the house, but held onto the door. She wished she had a better sense of what was happening and what was expected. Would she be spending the night? As friends or more than friends? Fuck. She brought her hands to her cheeks. *Get yourself together, girl.*

When she found Connor in the living room, he had already dispensed with his suit and was now sporting a faded blue t-shirt that looked like it had been sitting in the back of a closet. Pajama bottoms covered in snowmen hung low on his hips. She might have thought it was a completely different person if not for the hair, still perfectly in place.

"Everything sorted out with Alex?" he asked.

"All set." She scanned the tower of rumpled and devastatingly sexy man. "I see you're ready for a cozy night."

He pulled at his shirt and grinned. "Yeah. Got out of the suit pretty quick."

The two slow steps he took toward her felt like they lasted a year each. He reached out his arm and brushed the bare skin of her arm, sending goosebumps across her flesh. "Would you like to change?"

Short circuit was imminent. "Uhhh, okay."

Long fingers closed around her hand. "Come with me."

They wound through the open spaces of the large house to the bedroom she'd been in only days before. A door she hadn't noticed opened into a large closet. A sea of dark suits surrounded her from every direction.

Her fingers grazed the sleeves. Those suits had elicited such disdain from her and now all she wanted was to wrap herself in every single one. "Am I going to wear one of your suits?"

He frowned at her and opened a wide, shallow drawer. Perfectly stacked like shingles were dozens of t-shirts. Arranged by color, of course. She picked a white one with an intricate logo she didn't recognize.

He held it up. "Aaaah, my favorite bar in Georgetown. Nice choice."

She took it from his hand. Her first instinct was to dip her head down and bury her face in it. But she'd have to wait until he left the room.

He opened a deeper drawer. "Here are bottoms. And here are sweatshirts if you think you're going to be cold. I'll start queueing up the zombie movies. See you in the TV room."

Despite the fact that he was waiting for her, she took her time examining the closet that looked like an extension of the man. Large, refined, and orderly to a fault. It felt intimate to be getting undressed there, even though he was several rooms away. She hung her dress up, which created a crack in the homogeneity of the dark suits, and surveyed her underwear. She'd worn all the colors of the Virginia state flag. He knew about the blue of her dress, and maybe even the turquoise and amethyst bracelet. But the red lace underwear was a surprise she hoped he'd also see.

She put on her new outfit, turned off the closet light, and stepped into the now darkened bedroom. She had already slept in that bed, but not in a real way. Everything pointed to something different happening that night. She squeezed one of the pillows, so many desires crowding in her head. Was it wrong to wish her head would end up on that pillow, with his next to it?

Feeling about eight years old, she shuffled out of the bedroom in clothes that were several sizes too big for her. His eyes followed her every move as she approached.

He stared, then he laughed, then he stared again. "I thought the primary results were the best thing that happened today. Boy, was I wrong. You... wearing that... is the clear winner."

She snickered. "In case you don't recognize the look on my face, it's a complete lack of appreciation for your attitude."

"I'm sorry, Jenna," he said without a drop of remorse on his self-satisfied face. "Are you comfortable?"

She couldn't lie. Everything was so soft and smelled good and felt great. "Yes."

"Good, I'll try not to laugh."

She sat down next to him on the couch and tucked her legs underneath herself. Every few seconds, he chuckled, while she waited for him to pick up the TV remote and start the movie. Instead, he just kept staring.

"There's definitely something missing from this outfit."

She rolled her eyes. "Are you really starting again?"

"No, I mean, this." He ran his hand over her hair, still tied in a tight low bun. "Can I take it out?"

"Sure." Her voice shook. She turned her back to him.

With the care of a surgeon, he extracted one bobby pin at

a time, each making a tiny little click as he lay it on the coffee table.

"Wow, how many of these does it take to hold up your hair?"

"You'll see."

One by one, they came out until the mass of blonde waves came tumbling down. He ran his fingers across her scalp, massaging from the top of her head to her neck. An involuntary moan escaped her.

"I would have a perpetual headache if I had to do that everyday."

His talented fingers moved down to her shoulders, rubbing with enough pressure that pain mingled with pleasure.

"How come you never wear your hair down? I can't remember ever seeing it. And it's beautiful. Your hair is... beautiful." His voice had softened to a whisper.

She pulled away, partly because she was having ideas about where she wanted his hands to go next and partly because she wanted to see him. The eyes behind the thick-framed glasses locked onto hers. "It's more professional that way. And it's not what I want people to focus on."

He ran his hand over her hair again, as if he couldn't believe it was real. A knock on the side door made her jump. He slowly unwound his fingers from her mane.

Alex had arrived with the supplies and they both got up to greet him in the kitchen. He stopped dead in his tracks when he saw Jenna, and unsuccessfully attempted to hide his surprise.

"It's okay, Alex. Connor has already laughed at me quite a lot."

"I mean no disrespect, Ms. King. It's just... well, you look comfortable and happy. And beautiful as ever."

Connor took the bags from Alex and placed them on the counter. "Doesn't she?"

Those words nearly reached out and touched her, so warm and full of promise.

Alex handed her the card she'd given him, along with a small stack of receipts.

"Thank you so much, Alex. We'll see you on Thursday afternoon."

Connor stopped unpacking their dinner. "One day off? That's all we get?"

"Listen, I delayed the de-brief to give you an extra day of rest. But we've got a lot of work to do. This is the new starting line. Every moment counts."

Connor shook Alex's hand. "You heard the boss. See you on Thursday. And give Maggie our love."

"Yes, sir."

JENNA RIFLED through the remaining bags looking for perishables. Then a sense of warmth covered her entire back, causing her to stop. Although she wasn't wearing less than normal, something about being in his clothes made her feel so much more exposed. The presence of his body sharpened against her. She elbowed him softly in the stomach. "Hey, you're crowding me. Why don't you put some of this stuff away?"

Instead of stepping to the side of her, he reached past her, caging her body in even more. The hard muscles of his chest and abdomen pressed into her back and his chin grazed the side of her head. She held a bag of oranges in midair and swallowed.

He slid it out of her hand. "Okay, okay..."

She didn't look back as he brought the bags over to the

fridge. She'd have to get her head straight if she was going to make it through this night without combusting. Although everything was feeling very cozy, maybe even intimate, she couldn't assume they were both thinking the same thing. All he'd spoken about was beer and bad movies. And scratching his balls.

She meticulously folded each of the empty bags while trying to talk herself out of vaulting herself toward him. His large hand on the center of her back gave her a startle.

"Okay, everything's put away. Let's eat."

A vision of his mouth exploring her body popped into her head. *For fuck's sake, slow down, Jenna.*

CHAPTER 19

*I*t was impossible to hide his boner in those bottoms. Jenna, walking around his house, in his clothes, erased any self-control he might have wanted to exert. He thought he might die when he took her hair down. Somehow underneath that woman, who'd always been perfectly groomed and perfectly dressed, was a goddess. An unbound, dick-raising goddess.

He'd heard all about wild Jenna, with her nose piercing, army boots, and bad-boy boyfriends. It took him by surprise when she showed up as buttoned up as all the other professional women he'd known, but the original image never left his recurring fantasies. Maybe, somewhere on all that creamy skin, he'd even find a tattoo. The large spoon in his hand crashed onto the table.

She froze while pulling out two beers from the fridge. "Everything okay?"

"Yeah." He cleared his throat. "May I serve you?"

She gave him a curious look. "Sure."

She probably didn't trust that he would know what she

liked. But he knew. He'd been watching, studying, learning for five months.

The pleasure on her face when he handed her the perfect plate proved his point.

"Are we eating in here, or somewhere else?"

The thought of *somewhere else* teased at his crotch. He never skipped a meal, but if she had offered to forego dinner and go straight to the bedroom, he would have jumped at the chance. "How about we take our plates in the TV room? I don't want you to have to wait one more minute before experiencing the zombie apocalypse."

She grinned. "I'm surprised I've made it this long without zombies in my life. Or eating my brains, as it were."

WITH PLATES ON LAPS, they sat and ate. Two more helpings left him satisfied. At least for food. She had seconds, but left most of it on her plate. He'd probably finish it for her while the movie was running.

The neckline of the worn t-shirt she'd chosen kept sliding off to one side, revealing a bright red strap that just about made him cream his pants. If he didn't know better, he might have guessed she was trying to kill him.

Thoughts about kissing her, touching her, showing her how much he wanted her, consumed him. His decision to take his time and be strategic was dissolving in her presence. He'd even resolved that if all they did was hang out as friends that night, it would be an okay start. He wasn't looking for a quick lay with Jenna and didn't want to ruin everything by scaring her off. But that fucking red strap sure was testing every molecule of his self-control.

"Would you like me to tell you about this movie or do you want to be surprised?"

She looked at him as if he were crazy, an expression he'd seen on her face many times before. "Is there anything you think I should know that would enhance the experience?"

Underneath all that hair was a brain that consistently impressed the hell out of him. "No. Everything you need to know is revealed in the movie."

She bobbed her head. "No spoilers, then."

He tapped on the remote control. He wanted her to sit back, so he could put his arm around her, but she sat straight up. Maybe she wasn't comfortable enough.

"Need anything?"

She hopped to her feet. "I'll get us some more beer."

He took the opportunity to adjust himself. The way things were going, he could easily pop out of the top of his pants. Thankfully, there was nothing sexy about the movies he'd chosen, which would help keep the situation in his pants under better control.

She handed him a fresh beer and took a swig from hers.

He smiled up at her. "Thanks for this. Did you know it's my favorite beer?"

That look again. "Of course. Why do you think I got it?"

Whoa. He hadn't known. "I saw the Twix, too." One of the only exceptions of the meticulous care he took of his body. Those crispy chocolate bars were as addictive as crack. Almost as addictive as Jenna Fucking King.

"Hey, we're celebrating, aren't we?" She put her bottle down and folded her legs. Her mile-long legs that could easily wrap around his waist and-

He dropped his attention to the remote and pressed play. He needed something else to divert his attention. Pronto.

CONNOR WOKE up in the middle of the second zombie movie

and realized he had nodded off. Jenna was typing away on her computer. He watched her for minutes before she realized.

Her fingers stopped tapping. "I thought you were sleeping."

He smirked. "I thought you were relaxing."

"Just getting a few things done. No big deal."

"No work tonight. Please." He moved her laptop away and pulled her toward him, the back of her body so close to his chest they were almost touching. But she held herself stiff enough to leave a fingers-width of separation. "Have you changed your mind about the zombie genre?"

"I can admit it's better than what I expected. And also not anything I would voluntarily watch."

"Well, I appreciate you sitting here with me. Involuntarily watching."

"I thought you were crazy for not wanting to celebrate. But this was perfect."

"I was sure you'd find this utterly boring. Wild, worldly Jenna King stuck in suburban Virginia drinking shitty beer and watching terrible movies."

"Maybe you don't know me quite as well as you think you do."

He urged her back into his chest, and she finally relaxed into him. He became poignantly aware of the rhythm of their coordinated breathing, of his arm around her waist, of the smell of her hair, like magnolias, the flowers outside his father's house.

"I've never had a friend like you, Jenna. I'm not sure I've ever known anyone like you. And I know a lot of strong women. I'm surrounded by them. But you are something altogether different. You're like this unbridled power, like live electricity all contained in a little bun."

"Even when the bun has been released?"

"Especially so." He ran a finger across the bare skin on her shoulder where his shirt had fallen away again. He followed the line of the red strap. "I keep thinking you're going to find all of this dull and banal, and you'll walk away." His other hand wrapped tighter around her waist and curled around her hip.

"I'm not going anywhere. At least not until you're the new junior Senator from Virginia."

Those words from her lips sounded like angels singing. "If I haven't said it enough, I want you to know how much I appreciate all you've done for me. I wouldn't have made it this far without you. You saved my campaign. And me."

Her head moved very slowly up and down. He wished he could see her face and judge how well she was taking this. For now, he had to rely on how she moved, how she breathed, the softness under his hand.

"Six months ago I hardly knew you. And now you're one of the most important people in my life. Is it weird to say that?"

Her body got so still, he imagined she'd stopped breathing. She exhaled before answering. "No, it's not weird." She paused. "Except that it is. I mean, it's all been so unexpected. And we are so different."

He ran his palm down the outside of her arm to her hand, resting on her leg, and wove his fingers through hers. "We have plenty in common. We both come from powerful families."

"Yes, but we went in opposite directions with that. You chose to carry the legacy and I chose-"

"To push against it. I get that, but if you look more closely, you'll see that I'm following in the political footsteps, sure, but my values are in direct opposition to what my family used to stand for. I'm pushing against it too."

"I guess." She didn't sound convinced, even as her finger traced the outline of a snowman near his knee.

"As for your allegedly rebellious ways, I think your family value is independence and creating something new. Your father pioneered the computer business. Your brother pioneered psychology. You chose a path that no one had any connection to. And did it in your particularly unique way. That seems pretty on track to me."

"Hmmm."

He hoped the slight jostle of her torso was agreement and not discomfort. Or maybe she detected the hard-on pressing into her back. "And of course there's the crazy fact that our best friends hooked up with our siblings. That's got to be statistically as likely as getting hit by lightning."

A breath lifted and lowered her chest, those perfect tits teasing his hand, just inches away. "Okay, I'll give you that one. Was it strange to see Ramona and Lucas together?"

"Yes and no. Not sure if you know the whole story, but there was no shortage of drama. Even when we were kids. Our two families were so close and then our mom whisked us away. Lucas never stopped loving her, but they had to go through a lot to get back together again. I'm just glad she's back home now. And happy."

"They seem like a perfect match. Just like Camille and Jackson."

"How was it for you having your brother and best friend fall in love?"

Her fingers wrapped around his thumb and squeezed. "Excruciating. They are the two smartest people I know, but they both had their heads up their asses. For ten years! They both thought it was such a big secret, that they were in love, but everyone knew." She exhaled and a bit more of her weight fell into him. "But I've never seen two people more perfectly suited to each other. I think building a friendship for that long created something unbreakable."

Something unbreakable. That's exactly what he wanted. For the first time in his decades of life, it felt like maybe it wasn't just a fantasy. The woman leaning into him could be his unbreakable.

It's now or never. "I meant it when I said you are one of the most important people in my life. As more than just my colleague."

A quiver grew into a tremor, but he couldn't tell if it was his body or hers.

"Yes," she whispered.

He brushed his chin across her cheek, moving her hair away from her ear. His lips hovered so close to her, he could feel the heat of her skin. "As more than friends." His mouth pressed into her cheekbone.

She slowly sat up and turned around, eyes blazing. He wrapped his hand behind her neck, she clutched a handful of his shirt, and their mouths collided. She pulled him into her with such force that they both fell back into the couch. His hands tangled in her hair while she opened her mouth to his greedy tongue. She pulled away and took a gulp of air.

He pushed himself to sitting and then standing, breath cascading in and out of him.

She grabbed his wrist. "I don't want you to stop."

He leaned over, slipped one arm under her legs and the other around her shoulders. "I wasn't going to."

CHAPTER 20

*S*he buried her face into his neck, her mouth leaving a trail of hot wet kisses, as he carried her to the bedroom. If they had sat on the couch one more second, his body hard behind her, his fingers making their way across her arm and waist and hand, she was going to explode. Everything ached, from her throat to her nipples to the fire between her legs. Nothing could stop her from being with this man.

He laid her down on the bed and hovered above her, those brown eyes imploring her to connect with him. She slid his glasses off and placed them on the night table, before bringing her hands to his cheeks. "Can you still see me?"

"I can always see you." He dropped himself on top of her, their bodies pressed together, grinding from mouth, chest, and hips.

Her hands swept under his shirt and pants, starving for any piece of flesh she could get. That body had nearly incinerated her eyes too many times. She needed it in her grasp.

He knelt and pulled the collar of his shirt over his head. A huge expanse of the most exquisitely carved chest and abs filled her view. She'd seen him shirtless a few times, but touching him was surreal. Not an ounce of fat on that body made every one of his muscles stand out. She ran her nail across one of his small brown nipples and he gasped.

"Unbelievable," she thought, not knowing if it came out of her mouth.

He placed his palm on hers as she ran it across his chest, pausing above his heart.

"Believe it, Jenna."

His words felt like a spark on kindling. Yes, she could believe it. She stroked along the bulge between his legs and his whole body quaked. She grabbed for him, hands pulling at the drawstring of his pants, the need for him growing hotter and more desperate. But the more frenzied she became, the more he slowed down.

"I don't want to rush this."

The rasp of his voice vibrated deep into her core. She closed her eyes and focused on his hand drawing up the side of her body. Everything ached for his touch. The men she'd been with didn't do slow. They were more of the wham-bam style. But Connor wasn't just some guy. She could wait.

His fingertips skimmed the underside of her breast, then over it. He squeezed, and she clenched the pillow behind her.

"I've been waiting to see what that red strap was connected to all night."

A large hand tilted her up while his t-shirt was pulled over her head. He dipped down and grazed her collarbone with his teeth and then pulled the top of her breast into his mouth. Her hands clasped his face. He looked up, eyes capturing her while a finger traced along the low edge of the lacy cup. He never broke contact as he lifted her breast and cupped it. As he rolled her nipple between his fingers. As he finally unclasped her bra. Then his face was down, kissing her, sucking her, with soft bites and low growls.

She tipped back onto the bed as his mouth moved down her belly. One hand pulled the long string holding up her pants while the other grabbed the fabric and drew it down her legs. Waiting had become excruciating, but he showed no signs of speeding up. She began to slide off her panties, desperate for him to touch her, fuck her. He clasped her wrist and pinned it above her head.

An inferno lit his eyes. "I'll take care of you. I promise."

She squirmed but did not try to free herself from his hold. He ran his fingers over her panties and she yelped. Even through the fabric she was so sensitive it felt like he was electrified.

He examined her face. "Will you come like this? If I touch you?"

It felt like she might come even if he didn't touch her. "I... I think so."

He released her wrist and used both hands to remove the final item covering her. He kept his face just above her pussy and she squeezed her eyes, nearly overcome by the heat of his breath and the light touch of his fingertips.

When he bit the inside of her thigh, she clutched a handful of his hair and growled.

"Fuck," he breathed against her before turning his head, the bristle from his chin rubbing against her thigh.

Her eyes snapped open to see what had happened. She knew that look—eyes closed, breathing slowly, a rhythm playing out in the movement of his head.

She ran her hand gently through his hair. "Are you..."

He vaulted to the top of the bed and looked her straight in the eye. "I'm so fucking turned on, I'm about to blow. And I'm not ready for that. Not for a long time."

She pulled his mouth to her and wrapped her arms around his shoulders, kissing him with every drop of desire coursing through her. He slid his thigh between hers and she ground on him. The more she pushed against him, the more pressure he gave her. His tongue lapped at her, his lips pulled hers into his mouth, and all the time she rubbed herself against him.

When her breaths were coming sharp and fast, he slipped his hand where his thigh had been, one finger flicking her clit and others plunging into her, filling her so deeply she thought they would come out of her throat. She yelped and he slowed down, running his fingertips between her folds. Keeping constant pressure with the pad of his thumb, he entered her again, this time with smooth, even strokes, pressing in and up, until he carried her over the cliff of her orgasm. She groaned into his neck and clenched around him, each second expanded a hundred-fold.

He drew his fingers out of her and gently cupped her as she caught her breath.

"Connor." His name floated from her mouth to his as she closed any space between them. "That was amazing."

"God... Jenna..."

His whisper fanned her desire. She pulled at his pants until they fell past his hips, liberating a huge, rock-hard, stick-straight cock that looked straight out of a porno. She should have guessed that everything about this man was long and hard and beautiful to look at. He perched up on one elbow, hand still tucked between her legs, as she reached out to touch him.

Her fingertips grazed the deep V that dropped from his abdomen, to a patch of clean shaven silky skin. Sounds of pleasure came out of his open mouth as she curled her fingers behind his balls and cradled them. Her other hand took the bead of liquid on the top of his wide head and spread it in small circles.

When her fingers wrapped around his shaft, he clutched her hand with his, stopping her movement. "Does that not feel good?"

"Too good."

She wanted to tell him how often she'd thought about being together like this. How wonderful he'd made her feel. But complex thought was currently unavailable. "Let it be too good."

He loosened his grip and she stroked him, while all his remaining composure dissolved.

She could have waited. Could have been satisfied with how wonderful it had already been. But she wanted him, completely. Even if she couldn't possibly say the words—not yet—she could show him. "Do you have a condom?"

Brown eyes snapped open. Maybe he'd been thinking they would stop there. A moment of awkwardness bristled through her.

He ran his thumb across her lips and nodded before kissing her with the softest, most delicious mouth she'd ever kissed. "I didn't want to presume," he said.

She'd never been with a man who didn't presume. In fact, on a few occasions, they'd presumed too much. Of course, Connor was a gentleman. She wondered, if she asked him to, if he would stop being a gentleman. Then it hit her: maybe she wouldn't need to.

He rolled to the other side of the bed and opened the top drawer of the nightstand, returning with a black foil packet. Magnum, of course.

She took it out of his hands and watched the most incredible expression take over his face. Like surprise and delight and gratitude all wrapped up into one. Following his lead, she took her time rolling it onto him.

"You have an IUD, right?"

How did he know that? "Uh, yeah. How-"

"I felt it. With my fingers."

She winced. She didn't realize fingers could reach up that far. No wonder it felt like they were up by her throat.

"That's good. I don't like to only have one form of contraception."

Her brain tripped. "You... what?"

"You can't be too safe."

Of course he was right. He perched above her, a look of concentration on his face as he spread her thighs apart with his own. An exhale rushed out of him as his broad head made contact. And then all of a sudden it got very real. She closed her eyes.

"Will you look at me?"

Fuck. She didn't know if she could. It was feeling like too much. Too intense, too important, too meaningful.

He backed away from her, putting inches between them. The pressure between her legs disappeared. "Jenna."

She opened her eyes and tried to steady herself, emotion warming her cheeks.

"We don't have to. It's okay. I wasn't expecting anything. I promise."

"I want to, Connor. It just feels... big."

He looked down his body and then back at her.

"No, I didn't mean *that*. I mean..."

"It *is* big. And I don't mean my dick." His expression was as serious as night.

He reached down and she thought he would take off the condom so she grabbed his forearm. "No. I don't want you to stop. I'm just not used to being like this..." She was making no sense and she knew it. "I want this. I want you."

She directed his hips toward her. He didn't resist. The first sensation of him entering her caused them both to gasp. And as she struggled with the overwhelming fullness of him, he held her. With his unwavering gaze, with his deliberate patience, with the whispered poem of her name.

"Jenevieve..." he repeated until the rhythm carried her away from the edge of too much and back to him.

The muscles of his back rippled and pulsed as he controlled every thrust, every angle, every shift of her hips and legs. His body stayed as taught as a violin string, their moans a symphony of pleasure.

He lifted from her lips and dropped his forehead to hers. "You can't imagine how good this feels."

Her hands found the hard muscle of his bottom and brought his hips crashing onto hers. "I can."

"God," he cried out, all his tension bristling against her softness.

"Let go, Connor. Please."

As if a dam had been lifted, he rushed into her, so deeply she felt it from her navel radiating in all directions. He'd been unleashed. His arms wrapped around her neck and back as she spread her arms and legs and let herself be carried into an explosive collision of their orgasms. As open, trusting, and free as she'd ever been.

When his groan overtook her, she cried out for him, closed her arms around him, dug her fingers into his back as pulse after pulse joined them.

As she lay, fully enveloped by him, hovering in a sense of

satisfaction she hardly recognized, she became aware of three things.

1. Connor Barrett was good at many things. Exceptionally talented, even. But what he had just done, in that bed, could only be adequately described as a superpower.

2. Achieving that ever elusive second orgasm was merely a matter of deliberate, patient, persistent generosity. In other words, the right man for the job.

3. She might have, for the first time in her thirty years of life, experienced the difference between making love and fucking.

And maybe even a fourth thing.

4. Now that she had completely unlocked the door keeping her feelings in check, it was going to be nearly impossible to return to the way it was. And when all of this was over, and he was firmly situated in the US Senate, it was going to be unbearable to say goodbye.

CHAPTER 21

*C*onnor might have been crushing her, but the idea of separating from her was unthinkable. Even after their bodies had stilled, their breathing had slowed, and some of the heat had dissipated, he clung to her. She must have shared the feeling, as the grip of her arms and legs around him didn't loosen.

Reluctantly, he pushed up just enough to shift his weight to the side. His hand slipped between them as he gripped the edge of the condom and pulled out of her. A soft, sweet, sigh escaped from her ruddied lips. He'd tried to be gentle with her, but maybe near the end, when she'd asked him to let go, he'd gone too far. Something about her energy had felt so fragile, all her strength and power melting underneath him.

In his fantasies about Jenna, it had been completely different. Faster, harder, more raw and primal. There's no way he could have done it like that, no matter how much he had wanted to. He'd never imagined the sense that he might break her, but it was so clear in her body, the look on her face, the way she clutched him like a lifesaver. She'd called his name, pleaded with him to let go, but it felt much more like she was telling herself.

Yet one more thing that made her so intriguing. This wild woman, who looked like a doll, acted like a boss, and was something entirely different under his touch, awakened every single fiber of his being. Made him want to be inside her so fully that there was nothing about her he didn't know. And nothing about him that she didn't know. They could mold themselves together so strongly that they would be unbreakable.

He fell asleep with her hair curled around his fingers and the sound of her whispering his name.

THE SKY HAD JUST BEGUN to brighten when he slipped out of bed, put on a pair of shorts and headed down the stairs. There was no way he was leaving the house to meet Lucas for their standing date at the gym. He wasn't going to be apart from Jenna for as long as she let him. His home gym would have to suffice.

He decided not to turn on the music, which he typically blasted, for fear of waking her up. She needed a good night's sleep more than anyone. And he wanted her well rested. They were going to be very active for the next twenty-four hours, if he had his way.

There were few things he enjoyed more than training his body, but that morning it was especially difficult to get into it. Any memory of the night before brought him immediately to half mast, and occasionally more. The thought of her exquisite body, bare just above his head, made it nearly impossible to appreciate the burn of his muscles and the pressure on his breath. He dropped from a final pull-up and bounded up the stairs two at a time.

. . .

A POP SONG streamed from the partially open door of the bathroom. Except it was her voice, not the radio. Never, in the months they'd spent almost every minute together, had he heard a hum, a whistle, even a quoted lyric from Jenna. She was full on singing. Top of her lungs, echoing around the surfaces of his bathroom. Not bad either, except for the song.

He pushed the door open a few more inches. "Is that Justin Bieber?"

She screamed. Loud. He would have as well except that his ability to coordinate his vocal cords had vanished at the sight of her, stark naked, rifling through his medicine cabinet.

Everything he hadn't noticed while she was underneath him, in the dark, was crystal fucking clear. The way her tits stood at full attention. The definition of her un-fucking-believable abs. The tiny strip of golden hair on her mound. The carved lines of her thighs. The-

"You scared the shit out of me!"

Since his ability to speak had not yet returned, he continued to stare.

Her eyes moved to the fabric stretching out in his loose shorts. "Uh... I was looking for a toothbrush. Not snooping. I promise."

He couldn't have given a shit if she'd stolen his social security number at this point. How was it possible that a woman could look like that? "I... uh... you..." Giving up on language, he pointed to a tall white cabinet, which she opened.

She pulled out a toothbrush, still in its packaging, and turned her back to him, her glorious ass on display. All he could think was how those perfect, tight mounds would look with big, pink handprints.

She peeled the paper and plastic off the brush and ran it under water. Without looking up from smearing toothpaste on the new green brush, she said, "If you're going to stand there and stare at me, I have to insist that you also be naked."

Connor pulled off his sneakers, socks, and shorts as if they had caught on fire. Then she pivoted slowly, raking over his entire body, complete with bobbing dick, pointing straight up, with her huge blue eyes. He stepped toward her, opened up the side cabinet, retrieved his own toothbrush and joined her in the odd experience of nude toothbrushing.

She hummed. This time, a song he didn't recognize. But she stood there, without an ounce of self-consciousness about either of their bodies, brushing her teeth and making music with her mouth. If his heart weren't beating like a bongo, he might have imagined he had died and gone to heaven.

Then she turned toward the sink, filled her cupped palm with water and bent over to rinse her mouth. Bent. Over. Her ass cheeks slightly parted, giving him a view that probably added ten years to his life. He could have sworn she even wiggled a little bit. His toothbrush fell out of his mouth and bounced twice before landing next to her foot.

"At least it didn't land in the toilet," she said with a grin.

She stepped out of the way of the sink and waved her hand toward the running water. Right. Rinsing his mouth. Got it.

He pulled two white towels from the tall stack behind him and handed her one. She dried her face and hands, then reached up to place it on a hook. That's when he first saw the ink, on the side of her left breast. He held her arm up and touched the simple purple flower held in a deep letter V.

"That's beautiful. What is it?"

She lowered her arm. "Can I tell you about it later? Right now, I think we have a more pressing matter to attend to."

Her gaze dropped down to his boner, which had been staring up at her the whole time. Within a breath, their bodies were smashed together, hands and mouths on a frenzied grab for any piece of flesh. He picked her up, her endless legs wrapping around him like a vice and perfect handfuls of ass in his palms. Her wetness coated his stomach. For fuck's sake. It would have been the easiest thing in the world to back her up against the wall and plunge into her. But he couldn't. He hadn't slept with a woman without a condom since he was seventeen years old. And that had scared him sufficiently to not want to ever do it again.

"I'm so fucking ready for you, Connor."

If he hadn't been afraid of dropping her, he would have let his knees buckle. Maybe she wasn't the one in danger of breaking. "I have to get a condom."

She released her legs and stood up. Her palm scrubbed down her belly and stopped between her legs. "Get a few."

He'd never moved that fast in his life—across the bedroom to the nightstand drawer and back with condoms bursting from his clenched fist. She flattened her back against the doorframe, arms above her head. It didn't matter that he had no idea what she was preparing for, or that he couldn't figure out how to rip open the foil packet, she was just so amazing to look at.

"Allow me." She took the mangled packet from his hand, ripped it open, and rolled it onto his cock that was so hard he considered the possibility it might shatter.

He pulled her in to his body, all the soft, hard, sleek lines and curves mashing into him. He lifted her legs around him and she held onto the framing above them. Oh. It all made sense. Mind blown.

His fingers curled underneath her, finding a glorious slick of wetness. *Oh my fucking god.* He spread her open and brought himself to her. So hot he could feel it all the way to his balls. She clenched as he entered her. The look on her face read more like pain than pleasure.

"Jenna, baby. Is this too much?"

She squeezed her eyes shut. "Maybe. The angle is hard. With your... size."

It wouldn't have been the first time he'd come while only halfway in a woman, but it had been a very long time. He pushed her up and off him. "Stand up and turn around."

Everything in her face widened and brightened. He had no idea if it was going to work, having never been with a woman as tall as her, but fuck if he didn't want to try. She stepped inside the bathroom, turned toward the marble wall, put her hands up and bent forward.

He swallowed so hard his ears popped. His hands grasped her hips, about a million times more gently than he wanted to, and while pacing his breath to eight counts, entered her. Slowly, but not as slowly as the night before, he sheathed himself in her. Like dropping into a pool of bliss.

The skin of her back flushed while she bounced her hips off him. He couldn't look down; the view would have been too much. So he stared at the outline of her hand pressed against the grey threads of the marble wall. A hand reached back and clasped his, pushing his fingers even deeper into the soft flesh of her hips. When her thighs began to shake, he clenched his jaw so hard the ache spread across his skull, which held off the inevitable explosion for long enough to make sure she came first.

Despite everyone's belief about his rigidity, Connor tried to limit the number of rules in his life. This one—that the woman's pleasure came first—he wasn't about to break. Especially not with the goddess who'd gifted him with the best thing that had happened to him in a really long time.

When she called out his name and dropped the weight of her body into his arms, there was no question he would do anything for her. Anything.

THEY MOVED from the bathroom wall to the shower, and then, not wanting to get the bed wet and not wanting to stop long enough to dry off, the bedroom floor. Condom wrappers littered the area by the time Connor woke up, starving, but otherwise the happiest he'd ever been.

a movement in the bed pulled Jenna from sleep, and then his body was around hers. Strong, warm, delicious.

"Hey, sleepy head." His deep voice reverberated in her ear.

"Hey," she answered, so happy to be breathing him in. "Did you go somewhere?"

"I brought you some food."

She rubbed her empty belly, "Mmmmm. So good." She burrowed in a little deeper.

"You need to keep your energy up. I've got more... activities planned."

That might have even sounded better than the offer of food.

"I'm not going to stop loving you, Jenna."

As if an alarm had sounded, she went from groggy snuggling to wide awake.

He pulled away enough to see her face. "I guess you didn't like that."

Her heart was beating too fast. Don't. Freak. Out.

"I... it's just... " She dropped her gaze, now embarrassed that her shock had been so obvious.

He kissed her forehead, then the tip of her nose, then her lips. "Don't worry. It'll all get tucked right back into that bun of yours. But for now," he rolled on top of her, "the hair stays down, and you get used to me saying that word."

There was nothing she wanted more than hearing those words, except perhaps for saying them herself. She separated her legs and guided him between them. "I'd rather you just show me."

Food would have to wait.

LAYING in a postcoital stupor that felt more like intoxication than exhaustion, Jenna looked out the bedroom window to the dusky sky. She couldn't believe they'd been fucking and sleeping and fucking some more all day. Everything was raw - her lips, her breasts, between her legs - but she had no interest in stopping. Tomorrow would bring a different day and a set of challenges she hadn't yet figured out how to maneuver. For the moment, the only unanswered question was what flavor of pleasure they were going to enjoy next.

"I could just watch you, for hours and hours..." His voice tugged her toward him.

She closed her eyes and bathed in the warmth coming off his body. It seemed impossible that just one day ago, they hadn't even kissed. And now, she'd given Connor Barrett free reign on every square inch of her flesh. Even better, he'd given her access to his. Amazingly, his hotness went so far beyond that amazing physique of his. Connor had skills. Mad skills.

He ran a hand across her breasts, sending a tingle between her legs, then slipped it under her arm. "Tell me about this."

His touch was so soft, it almost tickled. "It's pretty new.

Got it around Christmas last year. Sometimes I forget it's there."

"Is it a violet?"

"Yeah. It was the name of my sister."

Shock filled his face. "Your sister? I never knew you had a sister."

"Yeah, none of us knew. Jackson found out by accident last year. Turns out my mom got pregnant before she and my dad got married. But the baby—Violet—died a few days old."

"Oh my gosh, Jenna, I had no idea. How sad for them."

She pulled at a blonde curl. "I always felt like I was supposed to have a sister. One of the reasons Cam and I bonded like we did. But it turns out I did and just didn't know it."

"That's a nice way to remember her."

"It's more than that, too. The way my parents described it, it was the worst time of their lives. They were young and in love and this terrible thing happened. It almost broke them apart, apparently. But as the years went on, they realized more and more what a gift she had been. My mother's family would have never let them get married if she wasn't pregnant. They tried to stop it, regardless. And then my parents decided to have a large family, which neither of them thought they wanted. It made them stronger, as a couple, more committed, more loyal, more grateful of the little things.

"When they told us about this, I was floored. I mean, I knew my parents had an amazing marriage. And I knew they'd gotten lots of shit from my mother's family. But the way they transformed that tragedy into something beautiful was just the most inspiring story I'd ever heard. That's what I want for my life. The ability to recover from hard things and be better than I was before."

Admittedly, there might not be anything better than how she currently felt.

He tipped her chin up to look at him. "I want that for you too, Jenna. Light on the tragedy, though."

His warm palm moved back over her chest, giving her breast a soft squeeze, then continuing down over her belly, where it stayed. "Your body is... unspeakable."

As much as she wanted him to continue down, another need made itself known. "Feed me."

His laugh surrounded her, from the vibration of the bed to the movement of his hand. "I'd love nothing more. We're a bit short on supplies, though. I'll head out to the store."

No way. "You can't do that. You're still the man-of-the-day."

He fell back into the pillow. "I'm not sure I'll ever be man-of-the-day, but I get your point. I'll ask Alex to pick us up a few things."

She shook her head. "No, I promised him a full day off."

"Yeah, you're right."

"Let's go to the kitchen. I'll take a look at what's left."

She got out of bed but realized at the doorway that he wasn't behind her. His lanky frame was stretched out on the rumpled bed. Damn, he was nice to look at.

He slid his arms behind his head.

"Are you coming?"

A grin filled his beautiful face. "I'd like to watch you walk away, if that's all right."

She shook her head and smiled. If a view was what he wanted, a view was what he'd get. She rose up on her tiptoes and pivoted in slow motion. He gasped as she took her first few steps, fingers palming her own ass, hips swaying. God, this was fun.

· · ·

JENNA LAID her head on his chest and walked her fingers across the expanse of his rippled abs, watching the room slowly fill with light. One more minute, she told herself, over and over. She needed so many more minutes.

He got up with her and made coffee. It had been so fucking hard to get out of that bed and face the actuality of real life. They had to get back to work. Of course, Connor wasn't making it easier by refusing to put anything on. Every glimpse of his breathtaking body was like an orgasm switch.

She did the best she could, getting dressed with another of his t-shirts and a pair of shorts. She'd only have to get in and out of the car, and back to her house to retrieve a proper outfit. Alex would probably have thoughts about her appearance, but he would be as restrained and professional as always.

Her hair gathered in a messy bun instead of her normally sleek one, she waited in the kitchen for the sound of the garage door opening. Connor brushed his palm across her cheek. "I need more time."

Every cell in her body screamed to cancel the whole thing, strip off her clothes, and get back into bed with him. But she couldn't. "We have to go, Connor. Eye on the prize, remember?"

Not that she had any idea what the prize was anymore, except that she was probably looking at it.

His lips tightened in an expression that looked a lot like frustration.

"Will you wear your hair down today?"

She frowned. "Not possible."

He tugged at a few loose strands. "Why not? It's so beautiful, baby. I still don't understand why you've kept it hidden all this time."

She sighed. "If I had let my hair down, I would still be

fetching coffee and making copies. I wouldn't be running your campaign right now. Your *winning* campaign."

He curled his lip. "That's ridiculous. Your competence would have-"

"Nope." She shook her head vigorously enough that hair went everywhere. "Tell me what you see when you look at me. Outfit notwithstanding."

His eyes darted left and right. She knew that meant he was looking for a trick.

"I'm serious. Tell me, as honestly as you can, what you see."

He gave her a serious examination. "You are a stunningly beautiful woman. You look like a movie star or a fairytale princess or something."

"And what does a fairytale princess want?"

He pressed his lips together. Recognition brought a look of disgust to his face. "A prince."

"Exactly."

"So what kind of response do you think I get from people who think I'm a princess?"

"A crapton of unwanted advances and disrespect."

"Bingo."

"I really don't want to believe that's true."

"Connor, you had the ultimate fortune to be born male and white and rich. Add on tall, intelligent, and from a prestigious family and it would never cross someone's mind to diminish your standing. They might not like you, but it will be taken for granted that you deserve any power you wield.

"Now, I'm pretty lucky too. And also, it's very very different. For me to be able to lead our staff, I couldn't have everyone thinking of me as a delicate princess. Or a hot piece of ass either. Do you understand? Even if I'd rather show up in hi-tops and a ponytail, that will never happen. Putting my hair away is the equivalent of you and those damn suits."

"But I don't mind the suits. I love wearing them. They reflect my personality and make me feel comfortable. But it sounds like you have to alter your natural appearance in order to do what you want to do in the world."

A smile spread across her face. "That's how it is for women."

He staggered back. "That's horrifying to me. I mean, of course I know that there's rampant discrimination. I'm not an idiot, even if I've never experienced it, personally. But this, with you, feels so personal. It doesn't even make me angry. It makes me deeply sad."

"One step at a time, one leader at a time, we change it."

"Shit. It sounds like you're the one who should be running for office. This kind of stuff can't stand."

"That's not my path. It's yours. And you're going to do something about it. Because that's the kind of man you are."

The recognizable rumble of the garage door pulled the sad furrow from his brow.

"Which is why you need to cover up all of that manly goodness and get your fine ass to the office. So we can do this."

He kissed her goodbye. "Yes, boss."

CHAPTER 23

*W*atching Jenna leave was fucking hard. Like a kick in the gut. Connor did what he did best and held it in, but it felt like his body was shattering. All the magic they'd created over the past thirty-six hours wouldn't last outside of it. At least not in the same way. She wouldn't allow it, and he couldn't argue. Of course, it was best to continue to act professionally. He didn't need any more attention on his love life and away from the serious issues at the heart of his campaign.

But he hoped some part of their new intimacy could be kept alive while they figured out how to announce it, spin it, make sure no one freaked out. He hadn't even considered her family. Her large, powerful family who might feel like he'd taken advantage. Although that was far from the truth. He hoped it was far from the truth. A boulder lodged itself in the middle of his chest.

No. Everything that happened between them was consensual. He had taken it slow, giving her plenty of time to back out, but she didn't. At all. She was in it as much as he was. And he was *so* in it. She was turning out to be everything he never knew he'd always wanted.

The boulder pushed up into his throat. How the hell was he going to go through a day without Jenna in his arms?

Every single thing reminded him of her. Every surface of the bathroom they'd christened, the bed, the rug, even the bench that normally held his worn shirts and on one spectacular occasion held her chest and belly as she folded over it.

Walking into his closet was the most difficult. That was the room she had first gotten undressed. No matter what had actually happened in that room, the scene he'd imagined while he waited for her would be forever burned in his mind. The red lacy bra and thong were layered on the fantasy after the fact, which made it even hotter. He hoped she had touched every one of his suits, maybe even put her face in his shirts. When she'd been in that room, he had let himself hope, for the first time, that they would be together.

He chose one of the new suits she'd helped him pick out. The one that had made those baby blues go big and bright. Maybe it would remind her how much she meant to him. How much he needed her. He was going to do his best to show her, even in the constraints of their professional relationship.

A beep on his phone alerted him that Alex was waiting for him in the garage. Connor almost canceled the ride and walked the few miles instead. As a compromise, he asked Alex to drop him off at the beginning of town so he could walk the few blocks to the campaign office. That way, he would have a bit more time to gather his thoughts before stepping through the door of his new life.

He was now the nominee and had many people to thank. Each business on that short stretch of Main Street would get a short visit and his sincere gratitude. They had rallied for him, which brought a lump to his throat. If all he did was to make sure these folks could live in peace and prosperity, he would be satisfied with his life.

Sometimes the big dreams did nothing but take him farther away from that feeling. Working for the millions had a different type of draw than helping the brothers who ran his favorite hardware store change outdated zoning regulations. He wanted to know that whatever happened in his career, he would never lose that personal connection. It was everything to him.

He arrived at the front door of 118 North Avenue and paused. Through the windows, he could see the typically busy office now frenetic. About a dozen smiling faces rushed about, high-fives liberally shared. Even more *Barrett for Senate* posters and banners hung from the walls, in addition to dozens of balloons covering the ceiling. It looked like the party had been going on for two days.

There was so much to do. They had less than a week to pack up the office and move one town over. Luisa, who had done an amazing job managing the volunteers, had probably been on the phone continuously since his win, recruiting more people. He'd have to find her an impressive position if he won. But first things first. They had five months to take his primary victory and turn it into a Senate seat.

The first sight of Jenna, hair pulled tight, dressed in a tailored suit he hadn't seen before, made him crash to a halt. Now that he knew what was underneath that shell, what she was capable of, it keeping his cool felt even harder. Beaming, he pulled open the door and strode toward her, ready to pull her into his arms.

He caught her eye and met her smile with his own. As if in slow motion, her smile became a frown, then a scowl, accompanied by a vigorous shake of her head. He stopped in his tracks.

"Good morning, everyone."

Every person in that room stopped what they were doing and faced him. With only a heartbeat of a pause, they all burst into applause. It would have been wonderful, if not for the look of deep concern on the face of the woman several feet in front of him.

She turned away, and he watched the miracle of her composure take form. She closed her eyes, took a deep breath, and stood up straighter. He could almost see the shell forming and hardening around her, as if she was slipping into a suit of armor.

"He kicked ass, didn't he?!" She screamed into the excited crowd, which incited even more applause. Then he was swarmed by handshakes, pats on the back, and hugs.

She never moved from where she stood, so he got to watch her, trying not to watch him. "Thank you everyone. If not for you, we wouldn't be here. You guys are the ones kicking ass!"

He took the few steps toward her, while the room was still enjoying their celebration, and tilted his head toward his office. "Shall we?"

In the same way they had at the start of every day in the office, they went into his small office for their morning meeting. They had fifteen minutes before senior staff joined them.

He followed her into the room and closed the door. "So, what's on for today?"

She spun on her heel and glared at him. "You can't look at me like that, Connor. Not here. It's completely-"

He put his hand up. "You're right." He knew his easy acknowledgment would take her off guard. "I forgot myself for a moment."

"Maybe-"

"Because just a few hours ago, you were on top of me, screaming my name, with the most amazing look on your face. Like you were seeing God for the first time."

She swallowed, probably unfamiliar with the feeling of being stunned silent. Composure returned eventually.

She looked just like the first time they met. Fierce, unapologetic certainty. "If you ever speak to me like that, in this office, I will walk out of here and not come back."

He took his time in answering, assessing which approach would best serve this situation. He gave her his best *I hear you* nod before responding. "I would have thought you'd have a better sense of humor this morning. I mean, after..."

She bit her lip, which meant something was beginning to dilute the anger. Her expression softened. And then transformed into deadly seriousness. "It's hard enough, with the constant rumors about us, to maintain control here. You need to not undo all my efforts. And remember, my credibility here is not for my ego. It is at the heart of my ability to run a successful campaign."

In that moment, he wondered if it was actually her brilliance and dedication that most turned him on. "Agreed. It won't happen again."

They transitioned to official business just in time for the rest of the senior staff to enter the office and for the meeting to begin.

CONNOR SAT, fidgeting, in the backseat of his car, waiting for Jenna to join him. Ten hours had flown by, as meetings, celebrations, and packing filled every moment. It could almost be mistaken for the end of any ordinary day, when they would ride to their respective homes together. But this was no ordinary day, and the rulebook no longer existed. Nerves brought a quiver to his breath, which did not subside even after she arrived.

"Will I be taking Ms. King home first?" Alex asked.

Jenna had only just taken a breath and relaxed back in the seat. Connor was hoping to have more time alone to talk about their plans. Of course, he wanted to be with her, but maybe she needed a break from him. He looked over at her, eyes closed. Yes, she was probably exhausted and looking forward to having some time alone. "Yes-"

"We'll just be going to Connor's," she interrupted. "Working late on something."

Alex's smile beamed in the rearview mirror. "Yes, Ms. King."

His trusted driver, as usual, knew exactly what was going on.

THEY'D HARDLY ENTERED the house when she turned and kissed him. Like she meant it. Bags dropped to the ground around them.

She pulled on his shirt and brought her mouth to his neck.

"Oh, is this what you came here for?"

She stopped kissing him and looked up, concern flashing across her face.

He immediately regretted making the joke. "Because I was going to tell you that I have no interest on working on anything other than seeing how many times you can come in a single night."

A breath rushed out of her body accompanied by a flush in her cheeks. He picked her up and set her down on the edge of the kitchen counter. Her hands assaulted his belt. It felt as if she had been waiting for this all day, as if she had barely contained her desire. It made him hard as a rock.

He lifted her skirt and slid her underwear down her amazing legs. It was the most delicate piece of black lace he'd ever seen. Right before his pants fell to the ground, he broke away from her ownership of his mouth. "I'll be right back."

It took him a few seconds to run into the bedroom for a condom and return to the kitchen, but she'd already hopped down off the counter. She took the condom from his hand, released the button and zipper of his pants, and dropped to her knees.

His groan bounced off every surface in the immaculate kitchen as her warm mouth enveloped him. He looked down to see her face, with his cock buried in it, and nearly exploded. That perfect face, eyes closed, focused on him. That perfect mouth sliding along his cock. Her hand cradling his balls and stroking him.

Stay cool, Connor. He closed his eyes and relaxed as her fingers wrapped around the base of his cock and squeezed. So fucking good.

She brought him to the back of her throat and he gripped the cold marble counter to steady himself. He had to stop her if he didn't want to blow his load.

"Jenna... love..." He gently pushed her away, immediately aching for her warm mouth around him. When she grabbed his ass, bringing him back to her, he did not resist.

No amount of willpower could contain the reaction she created in his body. In yet another example of his inability to say no to her, he let her suck him until his body had lost its bearings and his cum was streaming down her throat.

She looked at him with the most devilish look on her face. This was what Jenna-the-victorious looked like.

He slipped his hands under her arms and pulled her to

standing. "You look pretty pleased with yourself, Ms. King. Which I would agree is well deserved."

She wrapped her arms around his neck. "You've never let me finish before."

"Because I don't like to be done first."

"Well, I knew I had you at a weakened position today."

"That's downright diabolical."

She began sauntering toward the bedroom, that dream of an ass swaying just for him. "Whenever you're ready, I'll be hanging out near the doorframe. I have a good feeling about that location."

He looked down at his quickly returning erection. Only that woman was powerful enough to eliminate refractory period.

CHAPTER 24

*J*enna put her fork down and looked across the table at her aunt and uncle, chewing away. Even Connor, to her left, was placing a perfectly-cubed piece of zucchini into his mouth. She still hadn't gotten over the fact that the party she thought she was attending was just the four of them. It felt like a setup and the whole thing made her lose her appetite. Besides, she hated zucchini.

Uncle Robert lifted his hand and Penny scurried over. "Yes, Mr. Winston?"

"Please refill Mr. Barrett's glass."

Her eyes opened wide and she almost sprinted to the kitchen.

Aunt Olivia batted her lashes. "Such a sweet girl. And her mother was the best servant we've ever had. But Penny's a bit hopeless. I don't think domestic service is in her future."

Jenna's lack of appetite had become full-blown nausea. She downed her glass of wine so that by the time Penny returned with the bottle—if she returned with the bottle—her glass could also be refilled. A buzz might be the only way she'd be able to make it through this evening.

Uncle Robert lifted his newly-filled glass. "Here's to the newest power team in politics - Connor and Jenna!"

They'd already toasted. Twice. But, what the hell. Another excuse to drink.

"Jenna, dear, I can't believe how little we've seen you. Your parents asked me to keep an eye on you and I must admit I'm doing terribly!" Olivia cocked her head. Unfortunately, the amount of work she had done to her face made it nearly impossible to decipher emotion. "But you look well. Quite well."

"Thank you, Aunt Olivia. As you can imagine, we are so busy. And now that Connor has gotten the nomination, I don't anticipate we'll be slowing down at all."

Uncle Robert nodded. "Yes. You are certainly correct. These are going to be some of the most high pressure months of your life, I would imagine."

Connor put his arm around her, which nearly set her on fire. And not in a good way. He was supposed to keep the up-close-and-personal business on the down-low. They had agreed to hold off on the announcement, but there was his hand, on her shoulder, squeezing. "I'm just so grateful Jenna is here. She saved my ass."

Olivia's hand rushed to her mouth in a dramatic display of offense. "Connor!"

"Pardon my language."

Infinite barfing might be in her future.

"It is truly remarkable what you two have accomplished." Olivia said. "Especially considering that Jenna had no experience. None."

Jenna looked at her aunt, wondering why that particular emphasis was needed.

Her uncle twirled his glass. "What are your plans, dear,

after the election? I can imagine how many offers are in your future, if you haven't already received them."

Every fucking day. "Yes, Uncle Robert. Especially after the primaries. Lots of offers are coming in. But I'm not considering any of them."

"You... what?" Connor's dark brows perched above the frames of his glasses. "You've been getting job offers?"

Uncle Robert laughed. "Of course she has, Connor. Don't be naive. People are always looking for talent in this town and Jenna's a rising star."

This conversation might have surpassed the zucchini in distaste. She flitted her eyes at Connor's hand on her shoulder but he didn't move. "It's fine. I'm not entertaining any offers. I'm going to complete the job I came here to do."

"But what about after the election? I could see you running another campaign, taking a spot at one of the many political institutes, so many options for your future, my dear."

"I'm not sure. I didn't have a long term plan to re-settle in Virginia."

The hand tightened.

"Well, sweetheart, I understand that California is wonderful." The slight remnants of Olivia's drawl made a surprise appearance. "But Virginia seems to suit you. As does the thrill of politics. It's not as if you had so much going on back home, anyway."

Bloody hell. "Yes, I've enjoyed my time here, Aunt Olivia. I'm just not ready to make a decision yet. There's too much to do between now and then." Hopefully, that would close this infuriating conversation down.

She pointed a long pink-tipped finger. "If it were me, I'd never be able to return to such a small, quiet life after all this excitement. I mean, those little kids can't be nearly as interesting as all the powerful people you've met."

And this is why her mother had been glad to relocate across the country. Her family was the worst kind of awful. "I like simplicity. A nice quiet life can be wonderful."

The fingers around her shoulder stopped gripping.

Olivia batted her hand. "It's amazing how much you sound like your cousin, Lucas. He's turning down offers all over the world. Just wants to settle down and start a family. Such a waste of talent, if you ask me."

Lucas also happened to be an acclaimed chef, running two restaurants, and one of the happiest people she'd ever known.

"Now, your brother knows how to go after what he wants. That Jackson isn't going to be satisfied until he's got the world eating out of his palm."

"Yes, Jackson is very ambitious." What else could she say? There was no winning this conversation. "I have a single focus for the next five months. That feels like enough for me."

Her uncle reached his hand across the table. "Well, you know I'm happy to help you any way I can. Any introduction, any recommendation. You are my favorite niece, after all."

More like his only niece, but she still appreciated the thoughtfulness.

"Speaking of introductions," Robert continued, "we're all set for Wednesday's lunch, Connor. The guys are looking forward to meeting you."

The arm around her shoulder slithered away.

Jenna looked from one man to the other. "What lunch? And what guys?"

"I'm bringing Connor to the club to meet my committee members."

Robert was head of the House Appropriations Committee.

She gave Connor a face. "Oh, I haven't heard anything about it."

"I... uh..." *Nice comeback, Connor.*

Robert laughed. "Well, it's just the fellas, sweetie. The club, I mean."

She could not stand this one more second. "Are you kidding, me? Those things still exist?" She sat up taller. "Uncle Robert, it's very hard for me to manage a campaign if I don't know what's going on. It's imperative that I-"

"Sorry," Connor interrupted. "I forgot to let you know. But I knew you wouldn't be interested in that type of meeting."

Jenna swallowed about a hundred words, most of them profanity, and smiled. "We can talk about this later."

Robert pushed his chair back. "Hey, who wants to see my newest pin?"

Olivia wiped out her glass of wine and tapped her fingernail on the crystal. "We've all seen them, darling."

"I don't think Jenna has. Not in a long time, at least." He gazed at her like an excited child. "I've nearly doubled my collection. Come look!"

Without knowing what else to do, she excused herself from the table and followed her uncle to his study. He was right. It had been a long time since she'd been in that room and never noticed how much it looked like the library at Connor's grandfather's house. Or mansion, more accurately. Her uncle had been the protege of the former governor, but having spent her whole life on the other side of the country, she hadn't seen much of their relationship.

He opened a panel, then a safe, then slid out a shallow velvet-lined tray.

She stepped closer. A dozen or so ancient-looking pins with various campaign slogans were lined up underneath a glass lid. Pieces of American history. Much cooler than she would have expected. Before she reached over to lift the lid, he put the tray down on his desk.

"I want to talk to you about Connor."

Jenna looked up to his serious face. Oh, fuck. He knew.

"The way this has all worked out has been..."

She held her breath, waiting for something terrible to come out his mouth.

"Miraculous."

Jenna stepped back, nearly tripping over her own feet.

"After he fired Stanley Grayson, I was certain it was over for him. There was no possibility he could catch up after all that mess. Then you walked in, took charge, and brought him back. I don't know what you've done to that boy, but I've never seen him so poised for success. It's the comeback of the century."

"Thank you."

He shook his head. "I don't know if you knew, but his parents did a number on him. He fought his way back. And he's still fighting."

The depth of her uncertainty about where this conversation was going left her feeling very ill at ease. "Yes, I'm aware of that. But he's doing really great, now. I think he can take it all the way-"

"You see, that's the problem. I love Connor like a son. He's more like me than my own son ever was. I want everything for him."

"Yes, I understand."

"I don't want to see him thrown off course. Distracted by things that shouldn't matter. He's worked too hard to not make it all the way."

Jenna looked around for a seat. A sense of foreboding was

leaving her unsteady on her feet. "I'm not sure why you're telling me this."

He tapped a pen on his desk. "I want to make sure that you're giving him enough of a push. He deserves to have it all, which means eliminating the possibility of an easy option. It always disappoints him. He will be happiest if he can take his dreams as far as they go. If he compromises himself, gets confused by some kind of feelings, it will crush him." He bore into her. "You have his ear more than anyone else, darlin'. You need to keep driving him forward. Don't let him settle or get comfortable. You must not get soft with him. No matter what. Understand?"

Whether she did or didn't made no difference. She was going to nod and agree and get the hell out of that room. "Yes, Uncle Robert. I do."

All of that seriousness snapped into a wide grin. "I knew you would. He sure is lucky to have you. We all are."

She followed him out of the room, only remembering as he held the door for her that she hadn't gotten to look at those buttons, after all.

Jenna stopped at the bathroom before returning to join everyone in the sitting room. This evening had been a complete crapfest. She expected all that ugliness from her aunt, but her uncle was usually fun and charming. And then Connor with his arm and his secret men's meeting and his silence against all her aunt's insults.

She smoothed her hair back. There would be a conversation with Connor later but for the moment, it was her uncle's words which grated most. On the surface, she could have read his message as a simple request to keep urging Connor forward, which she was already doing. But some of the words he used didn't sit right.

Feelings. Distractions. Settle.

What she didn't want to hear was that her uncle had found out about their relationship. That he believed it would distract Connor. Make him soft. And if he made the mistake of choosing his feelings instead of his ambition, it would crush him.

CHAPTER 25

*E*veryone gave Connor shit about having a driver, but tonight demonstrated the precise reason why. He wanted to look at Jenna, figure out why she was so mad, but he had to keep his eyes on the road. With every minute they spent in the car, he could feel her pulling away. Yes, her aunt and uncle had said some crazy shit to her, but he couldn't imagine that she wasn't used to that. They were her family, after all.

Something had gone down during her private talk with Robert because when she got back, her eyes were blazing. Like she wanted to kill someone. Hopefully, it wasn't him.

He snuck a look. She was staring straight ahead, lip pulled in under her teeth. They might be just about to have their first real fight.

It had been going so well. Taking their relationship to another notch had been the best thing that ever happened. All he wanted was to be with her. At work, at home, in bed. Wherever she was, that's where he wanted to be. Except in this car, where it felt like a sheet of ice was forming between them.

PE KAVANAGH

She walked into the house, to the kitchen, and stopped. He paused at the doorway to the garage, waiting for her to do something. She stood in place.

"Can I get you anything, baby? You didn't eat much. Can I make you something?" He'd tried to keep his voice as steady and level as he could, but he was scared. She could turn around and just start screaming. Angry women had featured prominently in his life, even though he hadn't seen any of that in her. Maybe his luck had run out.

"Yes. I want celery and peanut butter. And tequila. I'm going to change."

She marched straight out of the kitchen toward the bedroom.

She returned wearing the t-shirt she'd adopted as her own. The one he'd won in the darts tournament when he was still in college. The material was so worn, it was almost translucent, which made it his favorite shirt as well. He could see every line and curve of that remarkable body of hers.

He'd prepared a plate with washed and cut celery sticks and a ramekin full of her favorite chunky peanut butter. It was definitely not a snack they shared, but he was happy to make it for her. Right next to it were two shot glasses, filled to the rim with her favorite tequila.

She looked down at the plate and nodded, then picked up one of the glasses and threw it back. "Are these both for me?"

Actually one was for him, but if she wanted it, she could have it. "It's yours if you want it."

She considered it for longer than he would have expected. Jenna wasn't indecisive when it came to tequila. "No. You have it."

It went down so nicely. If she wanted to do another, he would happily join her.

She took her plate and walked out into the sitting room, where she plopped onto the couch, balancing the plate on her crossed legs. All that bare flesh wiped his mind clean of any issue or problem. He would lick peanut butter off those legs like a dog if she'd let him.

The he remembered. He'd fucked up. "I'm sorry about tonight. I know a lot of things sucked for you. And why doesn't your aunt know that you hate zucchini?"

"You shouldn't have put your arm around me."

"I thought I played it off."

"I would have preferred if you had spoken up for me a bit more. I don't need you to fight my battles, or rescue me, but it was your fucking campaign we were talking about and you just sat there."

He wasn't sure he remembered all that. "When did I not defend you?"

"They were making all those comments about my future, about my plain and boring life, how I didn't measure up to Jackson. You didn't say a damn thing."

"That's not what I heard, babe. They were just pitching you the things they love - Virginia, politics, power, prestige. They just want you to be like them. That's their way of showing love." He knew, as soon as he said it, how fucked up that sounded.

"I'm not interested in having my life judged by them. So what if I want a small quiet life? How is it their business anyway?"

He bit the inside of his lip. *Don't take it personally, Connor.* "It's not their business. But they have a right to their opinion. Remember what you told me about not expecting people to only bring up the things you want to talk about? You said to control the narrative yourself. I know that's harder with family, but you could have done that."

She didn't look pleased, but he thought his point was logical. Maybe no one likes having their advice used against them.

"I've never felt good enough for them."

If only she knew all the glowing things he'd heard about her throughout his life. But that wasn't the point. "It doesn't matter. You know what you're doing and you know what you want. That's what's important."

She dipped her finger in the peanut butter, sans celery. Made his dick twitch.

"You didn't tell me about the job offers. I wish it hadn't been such a surprise to me."

"Because they're not relevant. I also don't tell you about every guy who tries to pick me up. It means nothing."

Ouch. "But it does matter. Even if you know you're not going to leave before the election, I'm interested in your life. I'm your friend." That was lame. "And no, I don't want to hear about the guys. But the other stuff, yes."

"You should have told me about the committee meeting."

"Yup. I should have, but I knew you'd be pissed and I didn't want to do anything to disturb you."

She stuck a plain celery stick into her mouth and took her time chewing. "I understand we have more going on than just a professional relationship, but withholding information in an attempt to not disturb me is fucking both of us."

"Got it."

She spun to look at him. "So, why did you think I'd be pissed?"

Now, they were getting somewhere. "I know you're uncomfortable with these backchannel dealings."

"Is that what this is? Some *turning the wheel* situation?"

He sat down next to her. "Yes."

Her breath became audible, as if she was tipping over into rage. "What the hell, Connor? Why are you doing this? All you did was rail against the way Stanley did things, and the way your relatives did things, and you're doing the same exact thing. What's going on?"

He didn't like those words coming out of her mouth. Not at all. "Hold on. You're taking this too far. Which is exactly why I didn't want to tell you. It's not some dark, elicit, or illegal plan. It's just how things work. But you get irrational about it."

He could almost see smoke coming off her hair. He braced himself.

"Irrational? You think I'm irrational?"

Instead of screeching or screaming, she stayed cool as ice. Which was infinitely scarier.

"At Uncle Robert's party, you were barely speaking to me, but made a point to tell me what your father said to you. You were clearly upset. About nothing. If you couldn't handle that, then being a part of what really happens, like at the committee meeting, would make your head explode."

She stabbed a piece of celery into the peanut butter. Maybe she was picturing his face. "What I don't understand, Connor, is how you rationalize your message of being transparent, in eliminating all the wheeling-dealing that always screws the people, of being a good person, with this behavior. Are you just lying to everybody?"

He wiped the glare that started to form on his face. Getting mad at her wasn't going to change anything. She just didn't understand and needed edification. Even though she was doing nothing but blaming and judging. "I feel like you're speaking from a position of ignorance. And I say that with huge amounts of respect for you, your intelligence, your morality, everything."

She put the plate down and crossed her arms. "Okay, tell me what I'm ignorant about."

He had to give her props for staying so calm. "I think you believe that one set of behaviors is moral and another isn't, where in reality they are both equivalent. And maybe you think I'm in danger of tarnishing some imaginary innocence. None of those things are true."

He had a flash of revealing the black mark of his past and swallowed against it. This conversation was headed directly to that piece of information. Not good.

"Bullshit. Of course there are moral behaviors and immoral behaviors. How is that under dispute? And yes, you have a pristine reputation. You're the rule-abiding, straight-laced candidate. No drama, no closet, no skeletons."

He would have understood anger from her, even confusion. But that's not what he read on her face. She was scared. What the hell was Jenna scared of? He was the one who had something to hide.

He stared at the pattern of the wood floor beneath his feet. If he was ever going to tell someone about his past, why not Jenna? She trusted him, and more importantly, he trusted her. She would understand. Hell, she'd already seen a tiny bit of his *behavior* issues.

"You think I'm so squeaky clean. I'm not. There are things in my past..."

The intense contraction in his chest forced a groan from his mouth. The pain was real. She could be repulsed that he was not who she thought, or who she wanted, and walk out of his life.

She got up off the couch. For a second, he thought she was walking out of the conversation, which nearly sent him into panic. When she returned with the tequila bottle and glasses, he exhaled a sigh of relief. She filled the glasses and looked at him. "You tell me yours and I'll tell you mine."

CHAPTER 26

*W*hat had she done?

Jenna had taken a difficult conversation about Connor's hypocrisy and turned it into her own personal confession nightmare. There was no reason for her to have made that offer. She could've just let him tell her whatever he was hiding. She didn't have to offer up her own. How fucking stupid.

The second shot slid down her throat, leaving a trail of heat but doing nothing to calm her pounding heart.

The whole point of a secret life was to keep it secret. Not to spill it the first time a cute boy made her feel all tingly inside. She'd become ridiculous.

He hadn't stopped staring. "I didn't realize you had anything to hide. I just assumed all your wild days were public."

"About as accurate as my assumption about you, apparently." She didn't want to sound curt, but fear was slashing her words.

He reached over and took her hands. It had worked so many times before, ever since the day of the shopping trip, when she'd gotten so nervous. It had become the balm for worry, stress, and fear. Whenever things got to be too much, he would gently, quietly take her hand and everything would be better.

It wasn't working this time. There was no gentle soothing, no calm in his touch, no understanding that it would all be okay.

He looked down at their hands. "You're shaking."

She couldn't look at him. Whatever was going through his mind—anger, confusion, concern—wasn't going to help her get this done. And even though she was as scared as she'd ever been, she was going to get this done.

For the first time, she was going to tell someone she cared about who she really was. It was ironic that it happened to be the person in her life who was beyond reproach. Pure, in a way more real than anyone she'd ever met. Brave enough to risk his entire reputation to defend her, then risk his ego as he cried in her arms. "I'm going first."

It was her only chance. After he confessed whatever minor transgression he believed to be unforgivable, she would lose her nerve. Knowing Connor, it was probably some parking ticket he'd forgotten to pay, or the one time he hadn't given back incorrect change. But hers was dark and ugly and personal.

"You don't have to go at all. I'm not asking you to reveal anything you don't want to."

Maybe he didn't want to know. Just like everyone else, who only wanted to see the blonde hair and sweet face and believe what they wanted to. There was no room in people's expectations of her for a dark swamp of ill deeds and a constant stream of hateful thoughts.

She pulled her hands out of his and reached for the bottle of tequila. He grabbed her wrist.

"Jenna, love." Panic lit his eyes. "I don't know what's happening. I feel like you're crossing into something really painful. You don't need to do this."

She jerked her arm out of his grasp. "I'm no fucking princess."

"Yeah... I... We talked about this. It's okay. I get it."

She took a long time to look at him, at his eyes behind his glasses, at the curve of his mouth, the cut of his jawline. Everything about him was perfect. But his went all the way through, unlike hers which stopped right at the surface. There was no way he *got it*. How could he? She had kept all of it so carefully hidden from him. From everyone. It's the only way her life would work.

"Maybe it's not okay. Maybe every time I have to hide myself, I die just a little bit. Maybe it's really not fucking okay!"

His lips pressed into a straight line. She could tell he was holding back all those questions popping in his brilliant mind. It was that same look he had when he was waiting to deliver a counter-argument.

He adjusted his glasses. "I never want you to hide from me."

If only she could believe him. "Everyone thinks I can't handle it. But I think it's them who can't handle it." She pointed her finger in his face. "I think it's *you* who can't handle it."

His eyes narrowed. "Handle what?"

"Everyone expects me to be sweet and pretty and nice. Anything else is unacceptable. How is that fair? It's like trying to breathe while someone is standing on your chest. If you only knew how different I am than what you think."

She could almost feel him pull away. Fuck him. So what if

he rejected her? Then she would know, instead of waiting until all her toxicity poisoned them both.

He dropped his head into his hands. "Don't do this. Please."

"Why? Don't you want to know who you're fucking? Probably not, right? Because it doesn't fit in your nice, neat, White-House-ready life. I look the part, but you and I both know that underneath is shit you don't want anywhere near you."

"Dammit, Jenna, stop it!"

She was startled by his raised voice. The first time he'd ever yelled at her. But it wouldn't stop her. "No, I won't."

He took her by the shoulders. "Don't you know that there's nothing you could say that would change how I feel about you?"

She pulled away. "Really? How about if I told you that I didn't come here because of you or my brother or your damn campaign? I came here because I'd made such a shitstorm in San Francisco that I had to leave. I was about to get fired from my job. They didn't really like me showing up drunk or sleeping with my students' dads. I couldn't walk into a single bar without a fight breaking out, just because of all the shit I pulled. I scraped by about a million close calls. Not that I deserved to. I was a one-woman wrecking crew."

She stood up and opened her arms wide, daring him to look at her. "Still think I can't change your mind?"

He didn't look disgusted, but she was sure it was in there. It had to be.

He slowly got to his feet. "I don't understand, Jenna."

Ha! Finally the truth. Here's where he would explain that she wasn't the woman he thought she was. That all her misdeeds had made her impossible to be with. Just like the others had. She folded her arms against her chest and braced herself.

"I feel like you *want* me to change my mind. Is that it?"

Her mouth opened and her arms dropped to her sides. He'd gotten it completely wrong. "No... I-"

"Or maybe you want to make it so that my confession won't seem so bad. Are you trying to leave me or protect me?" His head shook and his voice cracked.

Her mind whirled, trying to find an explanation. How had he so thoroughly misunderstood what she'd just said? "Did you hear me?"

He stepped inches away from her. "Yeah. I heard you say that you're tired of people thinking they know you because you look a certain way. That you did some things you're not proud of. That being treated like a princess who needs saving makes you feel like you can't breathe."

As the realization of what had just happened buckled her knees, she reached out to steady herself against him. Tears streamed down her face but she didn't let go of him.

"Did you think that would make me hate you?"

She pulled at his shirt, sobs bellowing out of her. "Why not? I've been a horrible person. You're supposed to hate me."

He moved one arm around her. Then another. "I don't hate you, Jenna. I love you."

Her weight dropped into his arms as it became impossible to hold herself up any longer. The words she least expected and most wanted to hear had just come out of his mouth.

Jenna tried to catch her breath and steady herself. She did not want to be hysterical. She wanted to look him in the eye and tell him how she felt, without a face full of tears and snot. But she couldn't stop crying, at this point unsure if it was sadness, relief, or disbelief. How could she have shown him all that horror and he still loved her?

"I... need... to ... sit... down."

He walked both of their bodies to the couch and sat her down on his lap. She curled her long body around him and cried a lifetime's worth of hurt onto his broad shoulders.

By the time the tears abated, his shirt was soaked and a severe pounding had developed around her temples. "I think I need some water."

In the next second, she was up, in his arms, heading for the bedroom. He put her down and strode out of the room, returning moments later with a pitcher of water and a glass.

She drank three full glasses.

He stood, watching her and rocking on his heels.

She pulled his arm. "Come sit with me."

He moved as if he was having trouble coordinating his limbs. Concern etched itself across his face.

She turned his cheek to face her and touched her lips to his. "I'm sorry. For hijacking your moment, and your confession. For utterly and completely losing my shit. For not believing that..." Tears threatened to steal her words again.

"You don't have to-"

She cupped his cheeks with both hands. "And I'm sorry for not telling you sooner. I love you, Connor. I love-"

And then his mouth was on hers, pulling her into him, making anything but loving him at that moment impossible. She held on until she was out of breath.

As much as she wanted to be taken by him, to release all the turmoil in her head by letting her body take charge, she couldn't let go of what hadn't been said. "I want to know what you were going to tell me."

He stiffened. "It's not important. Not anymore."

"No. You can't do that." It was important enough before her outburst. She wanted him to trust that she could handle it. "I want to know you. Please."

He shifted to the top of the bed and leaned back against the padded headboard. She slipped next to him and resisted dropping onto his shoulder. She needed a view into his eyes as he revealed what had been bothering him.

"I think you know about when I was younger, and I had anxiety issues."

She nodded and took his hand.

"It's been a long road, but I've mostly recovered, with some notable exceptions." His eyes darted away for a second. "It requires some discipline—explains a lot about why I live my life the way I do—but it's worth it to have emotional balance."

"I love how disciplined you are, without being judgmental and harsh." She ran her hand across his sculpted chest and abs. "Of course, I feel like I'm getting the benefits of that discipline, too."

A small smile temporarily displaced the upset on his face. "I love how you want me. Like you don't try to hide it in your eyes and in your body."

"I couldn't hide it even if I wanted to. You are... beautiful."

His head dropped. Not the reaction she was expecting. "I... I used to get into fights. As a teenager, even in college, but I forced myself to stop. Then..."

She reminded him of his words to her. "Connor, there's nothing you could say that will change how I feel about you."

He worked his jaw. "I had just started working as a defense attorney and was pulled in on a prestigious case. I don't know if they wanted my name, or thought I was any good, but I got this amazing opportunity. We were defending a powerful guy who was facing multiple counts of sexual assault. It was being framed as a smear campaign. He was a grade A asshole. Like a caricature: rich, powerful, entitled, dangerous.

"Then in one of his interviews, he started bragging how he wouldn't need all those other women because he'd been getting some from his stepdaughter." He winced. "He'd been raping his teenage stepdaughter for years."

Connor's breath grew raspy as he closed his eyes. This was him trying to regain control. It broke her heart to see him like this but she had to let him do what he needed to do. She offered tender strokes to his arm and hand as she waited.

"I was managing. I mean, it made me sick to look at him, but I was managing. And then one day, he slapped me on the back and said something like, 'Men will be men.' I lost it. I just started punching him and didn't stop. His staff had to pull me off him."

It was her turn to manage herself. She did not want to over-react. She nodded slowly and never released contact with him.

"I almost killed him. I could have killed him. If those guys had been one minute later, I would have."

"Holy shit, Connor." It slipped out and she bit her lip.

"I should've been arrested. Dis-barred."

Why hadn't she heard about something so dramatic happening among her family's friends? "What happened?"

"Nothing. My grandfather pulled every string he had. They made some deal with the defendant and the whole thing disappeared. So, he walked away scot free."

It was imperative she keep her expression calm, but she was losing control. "I'm not sure getting your ass kicked would constitute scot free."

"He got away with all of it, Jenna." His voice cracked. "Because of me."

CHAPTER 27

*C*onnor didn't blink, scanning her face for any sign of a reaction. She stayed as impassive as a statue. There was more to say—so much more—but he resisted going on.

"You don't have to pretend it's okay."

She narrowed her eyes. "I'm not pretending. I'm listening."

"I want you to know something else. When you get upset about what you think is happening with Uncle Robert, or your father, or me, it needs to be put in context. This situation, with my assault of a client, means I understand what it means to toy with the law. To shred it. And what I'm doing with Robert and anyone else is not that."

Her breath quickened, but he had still no idea what she was feeling.

He swallowed and counted, struggling to find enough air.

"I understand," was all she said before closing her eyes.

He knew it. His secret, kept for all these years, should have stayed buried. It was a miracle that it hadn't already exploded in his face. With all the people involved—the rapist, his family, lawyers on both sides—it could have easily come back to haunt him. When he decided to pursue public office, he was certain someone would use that situation against him, but so far, nothing. No blackmail threats, no extortion, nothing. Even so, it never left his mind.

He watched her, face so still she could have been sleeping. The waiting was killing him. It felt like a millennium passed before she opened her eyes and looked at him.

"I love you, Connor Francisco Barrett. I think you are an honorable man and I'm proud to know you. Thank you for trusting me with this."

Although the words were fine, the way she said them sounded like something was very wrong. "It's not okay, is it?"

She ran a hand along his cheek. "Please don't think that. I'm just absorbing what you told me. I never expected..."

Yes. No one ever expected. That problem, it appeared, they shared.

SLEEP WOULDN'T COME. After all that had happened, Connor's mind wouldn't still enough to let him fall asleep. Over and over, Jenna wrote out on his chest a letter I, then a heart, then a letter U. As if she was reminding herself of what she'd said before his secret had tainted everything. Maybe if he could wear it, like a brand, she wouldn't be able to take it it back.

"I've never thought about getting a tattoo..."

Her head popped up.

"But I'd get that one."

He looked down to her tired eyes and smiled. "Can't sleep, either?"

She shook her head.

"It was too much, right?"

She lifted up on her forearms and stared at him, a very clear frown on her beautiful face. "You're not allowed to do that. It wasn't too much."

He tried to smile and wanted to believe.

A spark flickered in her eyes. "Want to hear more of my dark secrets?"

"You have more?"

She grinned. "So much more."

They spent the rest of the night sharing as many secrets as they could remember, which eventually devolved into a competition around childhood antics. With every confession —Connor's sticking his finger in his sister's birthday cake, Jenna's hoarding all her friends' bubble gum—the tension in her body dissipated.

He watched her as closely as he had ever watched another human being. Everything he knew about Jenna added to the analysis of her feelings. She never brought up what they'd shared with each other, but he prayed this process of peeling away the parts of herself she'd kept hidden would convince her to trust him. It was true when he'd said to her that there was nothing she could say that would diminish his feelings. All her truth-telling only made hime him love her more.

He eventually fell asleep, face sore from laughing, and heart so full it nearly hurt to be contained in his chest.

CONNOR WAITED IMPATIENTLY for her to wake up. She finally blinked her eyes open and smiled. Without hesitation, she kissed him as if they had just a night full of lovemaking instead of dark revelations.

"Come away with me."

She rubbed her eyes. "What?"

"Ramona and Lucas are using the lake house this week.

Something she called a baby-moon, even though I think she just made that up. Anyway, they've invited us up for a few days and I think it's a great idea. We could use a little down time, and it might be the last chance before the election."

He could almost see the gears of her mind turning. They'd hardly slept and he didn't blame her for being slow. "I know what a baby-moon is. That's usually just the couple. No friends or family. Wouldn't we be on top of each other?"

He laughed. "You know how my grandfather left the mansion to Ramona?"

She nodded.

"He left me the lake house."

She nodded again.

"It's a comparable property."

Big blue eyes finally registered what he meant.

"There's plenty of room for the four of us. And it's my birthday."

She tried to hide her surprise. Maybe she hadn't remembered. "Yes, I... Do you think we can afford the time away?"

"I think we need to make the time. And I want to take you away from all this for a few days." The idea of being at the lake with Jenna sounded like heaven. "You know the whole 'Virginia is for Lovers' slogan? Well, most of those ads are based on my grandfather's property. It's beautiful up there. Unless you want to go some other time, when it's just the two of us?"

"No. I'd like to spend some time with Ramona and Lucas. And yes, maybe another time with just the two of us, too."

Now, that's what he wanted to hear. "Great. It's a date. We'll drive down on Wednesday and come back on Sunday."

"That sounds amazing." Something flashed across her expression. "Speaking of Wednesday..."

Right. One of the few issues they hadn't discussed last night. It pained him to have to go back. He wanted to be passed all of it.

"What are we going to do about the committee meeting?"

He liked the way she put it. *We* instead of *he*. "Would you like me to change the location so you can attend? Or would you like me to cancel it?"

"I don't want you to cancel it. And if you want to take the meeting without me, that's fine too. I mean, after you're Senator, you're going to be doing all this on your own. Or with your own advisors. Maybe I shouldn't force myself-"

"You're not forcing yourself." He managed his tone, which was reflecting how disturbed her statement had made him. Flung him from *in love* to alone. *After you're Senator* had always been Jenna code for *after I'm gone.* "You need to be there."

"I was just being insecure. The way it was brought up made me feel like I didn't know what I was doing. Like the important parts of the job were being handled outside of my control. But I know that's just the stuff in my head. I promise, I'm okay if you want to take the meeting without me. You'll be doing that soon enough, anyway."

He clenched and unclenched his jaw. There was going to be another conversation in their future. About their future. She needed to stop describing the election like the edge of a cliff. But it wasn't going to happen now. They'd already taken some major steps and needed to get acclimated. "No. I'm insisting that you attend."

Her eyebrows vaulted up as she tried to press down a rising smile. "Insisting?"

"Yes." He tried to keep a serious face. "I am your boss, if you remember."

The smile fought its way out. "Yes, boss."

Holy shit, did he like the sound of that. So did his dick.

"Excuse me, Mayor Barrett?"

Holy hell, she was teasing him. "Yes, Ms. King."

"I'm hungry. Is it time to eat?"

So many possibilities flashed before his eyes. Wonderful possibilities. But one rose to the top. "Yes. But I'll be eating first, if you don't mind."

And then, he buried himself under the blanket.

The moment his tongue slid between her legs she starting moaning. He had no interest in taking his time. She needed to come fast and hard and right then. He pulled her clit between his lips, slipped two fingers inside her and curled in. This was Jenna's magical orgasm switch and no matter how much or how little warm-up had preceded it, she came almost immediately. He preferred to take his time, to tease her until she was pulling chunks of hair out of his head and screaming bloody murder, but that morning, there would be no waiting.

She bucked up against him and clenched around his fingers. He didn't let up until all the pulses had stilled, her clit now a swollen berry held between his lips. He also knew she could come again if he let up almost all the pressure, but kept his mouth and fingers exactly where they were.

Her hands pulled at his shoulders. "Come up here."

Instead of an answer, he hummed, vibrating her whole core.

"Fuck," she cried out.

He hummed deeper and louder. She started panting, the craziest fucking sound he'd ever heard. Like pleasure being fed directly to his brain. When his tongue flicked her once, twice, a third time her thighs began to shake. His other hand, which had been steadying her hips, spread her open, giving him even more access. He swept his lips across her with excruciating slowness, knowing how that bit of stubble made her feel, especially when she was already so sensitive.

Her high pitched gasps grew deeper and more guttural. He considered drawing it out longer, but couldn't get himself to make her wait. He pulled in with his tongue, curled in his fingers, and she dissolved again around his very grateful mouth.

By the time he'd kissed his way up to her face, lingering around those mind-melting tits, she looked crazed. That look he would have captured and framed on his desk if every man on the whole damn planet wouldn't have known exactly when it was taken. Getting that response was part of his plan, every fucking day.

She grabbed for him. "You're on fire today, Barrett."

"I believe that's you who's on fire, Ms. King."

She wrapped her legs around his waist and pulled him to her. For this part, he was going to exercise plenty of patience. He was in no rush to get to his own goal line. He pulled her up to sitting, then onto his lap. Her eyes flickered with excitement. She loved this position. And he loved that she loved it.

He leaned back on his hands and she straddled him, nearly sliding him into her sopping wet center, before jerking away.

"Sorry," she said, with an expression he didn't like at all. He could only imagine what it would feel like to enter her, bare. But that thought threatened to ruin any hint of control. She slipped a condom on him, concentration narrowing her eyes, then perched herself above him. She loved controlling how fast and how deep he entered her, and he'd learned not to interfere. That is, until she needed him to increase the intensity and push against her.

With every inch, her face shifted. Her nostrils flared, her

eyes fluttered, her mouth opened. It was impossible to watch and impossible not to watch. Then she did that thing that felt like belly dancing or hula dancing or something where the woman deteriorates your control with her hips. She paused when he had fully entered her and smiled, waiting for his recognition that she'd taken him in. All of him. At which point he exhaled and nodded.

And then she rode the living fuck out of him.

CHAPTER 28

*T*hey'd passed a security gate miles before. Jenna kept looking for a house to appear out of the dense wooded hills, but nothing. "Are we going somewhere first?"

Connor gave her an odd look. "No. Headed straight to the house. Are you okay? Have to pee?"

She rolled her eyes. "No, I don't have to pee."

He squeezed her thigh. "Almost there."

She shouldn't have been worried about somehow missing the house, because a few minutes later a huge lake, fronted by an even bigger house, popped up in front of them. He'd told her it was a significant property but somehow she just kept picturing a quaint country cabin. This was no country cabin. More like a villa. Or an estate. Or whatever you call those things.

"Holy shit."

He laughed. "I told you."

"And your grandfather left this to you?"

"Yup."

"The whole lake too?"

He laughed harder. "No. Not the whole lake. The other

side is public, beach and trails. This side is private. Most of it is ours."

She tried not to linger on the *ours*, because those possibilities would be even harder to handle than the house.

They pulled around the gravel driveway, stopping right in front of an enormous entry. She squinted, because it was almost as if she could see right through the house. She stepped out of the car. Yes, the entire rear of the house, facing the lake, was glass. Holy mother.

"You go in, baby. I'll bring our stuff."

She stepped inside the empty house and realized, immediately, that Connor had been correct. She did have to pee. For the third time since they'd left home. It wasn't the coffee, or the water, or even that the ride had been particularly long. It was all nerves. This, on the two week anniversary of having taken their relationship to another level, was the first time they'd be going public as a couple.

Sure, she'd told Camille—almost at the moment it happened— and then Jackson, and Connor told Lucas, and then Ramona. But they hadn't had the chance to be together, as a couple, in front of their friends and family.

It was hard to predict what people's reactions would be. They'd received nothing but congratulations and good wishes, but family could be tweaky when they saw, with their own eyes, such a big change in people's behavior. They'd spent months vigorously squashing all the rumors of their sexual relationship and now here they were. Doing it. As often as they could.

As Jenna tried to use her divining skills to figure out which of the dozen doors off the huge multi-story foyer might contain a bathroom, Lucas rounded a corner.

"Jenna!" He rushed in for a hug.

"Hey, cuz. What's happening?" She patted his back.

He beamed down at her. "So great to see you."

Connor entered, laden with bags. "Lu-ser!"

"Con-man!" Lucas answered.

Ramona, probably drawn by the man-shouts, joined them, wearing a tiny sundress that featured ginormous boobs, a matching belly, and killer legs. Wow, that woman needed to have a dozen babies. She rocked pregnancy like a supermodel.

"Hey, you guys. You made it."

Connor planted a kiss on the top of her head. "Of course we made it. Did you think we would accidentally drive into the lake?"

She quirked a brow. "I know how rarely you drive these days, so I wasn't sure you could maneuver the winding roads."

She gave Jenna a big hug, while daring her brother to respond.

"Okay, Mo. First jab, landed."

Lucas picked up two of the bags Connor put down. "I'll help you bring the bags up, Con."

Ramona pointed up the stairs. "We took the Anna room. Figured you guys would want Beverly or Gail."

Connor picked up the remaining bags and followed Lucas up the stairs. "I'll work it out."

Jenna's bladder was about to explode. "Could you point me toward a bathroom. I'm about to wet myself."

Ramona laughed and pointed to a gold trimmed door. "Welcome to my life!"

JENNA EXITED the bathroom to find Connor waiting for her. "Do you have to go?"

He smiled. "No, darlin'. I was just waiting for you. Didn't want you getting lost."

She looked around the immense space. "Good call. Did I mention I was picturing a little country cabin?"

"I tried to tell you." He surprised her with a knee-bending kiss. "Have I told you how happy I am you're here with me?"

He had. Several times. "Yes. But don't stop, okay?"

He shook his head. "I will never stop."

She ran her thumb across his cheek. "Love you."

"I'm not sure when I'm going to get used to hearing those words from your mouth, but I don't think it's going to be soon."

"Good."

"Let's go out to the patio. Lucas made lunch."

THE NEXT MORNING, Connor was kind enough to let her linger in bed. After an hour of ravishment so complete she would've guessed that he would skip his morning workout. But apparently, he and Lucas had a routine of swimming the lake, which left her to luxuriate in that wonderful bed all by herself.

Ramona was tapping away on her computer when Jenna finally made it downstairs. "Good morning!"

"Hey, Ramona." She gave her a hug. "How's your morning?"

"Excellent. We got the satellite upgraded recently and the wifi is blazing fast. It used to be so painful coming here when we were younger and had no internet."

"Are you working?"

"A little bit. I get as much done as I can while Lucas is working out, then no more for the rest of the day. I want to make sure Connor's situation is solid before baby Winnie sucks all my time away."

"Gosh Ramona, I'm so impressed with you."

Ramona bellowed out a laugh. "Shit. Just peed myself. And I'm so far from impressive. Just wait till you see how much I'm going to flounder with motherhood."

Jenna seriously doubted it. So far, Ramona had turned out to be one of these utterly competent people. Like Camille. "You are going to be awesome."

"At least we're saving up for therapy."

They both laughed.

"So, I'm glad we have some time together. Just us."

Jenna's jaw tightened. This might be the sister talk she was expecting. "Yeah. Me, too."

Ramona got up to refill her glass from the thick brownish liquid in the blender. "I won't offer you my pregnancy smoothie. It's got lots of prenatal vitamins and it tastes like hell. Can I get you something? I think there's some coffee leftover from the guys."

"You sit down. I'll get it."

Ramona drew a sip up her straw and fixed her gaze on Jenna. "You and Connor look really happy."

Here we go. "Yes, I feel like we are. I know it's a big change, and might be weird for people, but we're happy."

"He told me he loves you."

Jenna accepted the small gift of already having filled her coffee cup. Otherwise, it might have been covering her. "Wow. Uh... yes. We are in love."

"I was surprised. You are so different than the women I've seen with him before."

Jenna tried not to bristle. Ramona was direct. "Yes, I've heard that."

"I think it's a good thing. A very good thing."

Jenna exhaled and nodded, unsure how to respond.

Ramona leaned forward. "Here's what I'm still worried about."

Relief had clearly come too soon. Jenna waited.

"For most of Connor's adult life, the two goals of his life have been the White House and love."

She'd never heard it put quite like that, but she couldn't argue. It did sum him up pretty well. "Yes, I-"

"For the most part, they haven't conflicted, and he's had much better success in one than the other."

Politics had been winning, as far as Jenna could see. Before her, of course.

"I want him to have it all. And I want him to be healthy. That's a lot of pressure on the person he chooses to be with. I guess I just want to make sure you know that."

Holy hell. She was hoping something much stronger than coffee would magically appear in her cup. "My commitment to his campaign hasn't wavered, Ramona. I think we want the same things for him."

"But how about your commitment to him, as a man?"

Ramona raised her hand before she could answer. "I realize it's creepy that his sister is asking that question. But I know he's fallen hard for you. Really hard. It scares me to think of what happens if things should go bad. It could all blow up for him."

Jenna forced herself to move past being offended and see Ramona's position. Grasp the bigger picture. "I can't guarantee the future. But, here's what I know: changing the nature of our relationship was something I took very seriously. And put off for a long time. We didn't just fall into bed together looking for a good time. I am well aware of the stakes for his future."

"But-"

"Please let me finish." It was her turn to take charge of the conversation. "I love him. We are very good together. Personally and professionally. I'm not sure if you're basing your concern on some preconception about who I am, or what I've done, but I hope you can see who I am, in front of you."

Ramona rubbed her belly and frowned. "Well, now I feel like a total bitch. I can see how what I said sounded really shitty. I didn't mean to offend. I'm just emotional and stressed and so fucking scared for my brother, it keeps me up at night. That and my bladder, of course."

Jenna had no excuse for the tears pressing against her own throat.

"You know, we're family now. Or about to be." Ramona reached out a hand. "I hope you can take what I said in light of my situation. And what we both know about Connor."

As Jenna formulated a response, the two men came into view, sprinting at top speed across the shoreline toward the house.

Ramona squeezed her arm. "Are we good?"

There was only one allowable answer. "Yes. We're good."

Jenna hugged her while keeping her gaze at the man coming toward them, chest heaving and shimmering with sweat. That man. Her heart somersaulted right out of that uncomfortable kitchen to where it belonged.

AFTER THE MEN recounted the story of their morning adventures, including getting yelled off the rock wall on someone else's property, and an alleged sighting of some sea monster, Connor pulled Jenna upstairs.

He stripped out of his wet clothes. "Did you have a good morning, babe?"

She considered how much to tell him. And then remembered. Truth first. "Your sister had some concerns she shared with me."

His expression snapped to apprehension. "What did she say?"

She wrapped her arms around his neck. "It's okay. She's worried about how our new relationship is going to impact the campaign. Don't worry. It's handled."

"I fucking love you so much."

Now that's more like what she wanted to hear. "What are we doing today?"

He grinned about as wide as she'd ever seen him grin. Like, scary wide. "We're going for a bike ride."

Oh, that sounded sweet. All the scenic roads in the area would make for a beautiful ride. It would be great to be out of the house for a bit. "You have a bicycle for me?"

"No. And it's not that type of bike."

CHAPTER 29

*C*onnor could count the number of times he'd seen Jenna King speechless on one hand. Two fingers, in fact. But when he brought her into the garage and walked her to his Ducati Racer, she could not hold her face together. Not even one bit.

"This is your bike?"

"Yeah. I only keep it here because traffic's too crazy near the city. But these roads, and this bike, that's a good match."

She reached out a finger to touch it as if it was a mirage or a hologram. Then looked up at him the same way. Blowing her mind, for the second time that day, made him feel like a fucking superhero.

He pulled two helmets off the wall and handed her one. "Are you okay with this?"

She faked him out with a shake of the head. Uh oh. "I just can't believe it. In a million years, I wouldn't have expected you... and this..."

That's right. He was planning on surprising this woman for as long as he possibly could.

. . .

HE HAD EXPECTED that this was not her first time on the back of motorcycle, but the way she held onto his waist and glued her body to his, made him feel like he might have been wrong, so he took it slow. He'd been carving those roads since he was a teenager, well before he should've been on the back of a bike. He could've pushed it without worry, but he kept tight control of the bike. Only when her body relaxed, the grasp a bit less intense, did he start to play with the curves. Part of what he loved about riding there was the fact that there was not another person or vehicle around. The worst they would encounter is a brave squirrel.

When he heard her whoop excitedly at the view of the lake, now well below them, he decided to try one more thing.

He pulled over to a lookout, took off his helmet and hers, and walked over to the vista. They stood hand-in-hand watching the still water, cut by the occasional yacht, and the nearly endless tree-covered hills.

Her eyes widened as if they might swallow the whole scene. "So beautiful..."

"Virginia is for lovers."

She gave him a slap on the belly. "Yeah, I heard that somewhere."

"Have you ever ridden without a helmet?"

She gave him her best incredulous look. "No, of course not. The law's been in effect in California my whole life."

He took her hand. "Would you like to?"

All sorts of confusion crossed that beautiful face. "What? How?"

"This is all private property, so it's not illegal."

More confusion. "Wait. Are you saying all this property is yours?"

"Yes. Anyway, if you'd like to, we can. It's an amazing feeling. And, I promise I'll go slow."

She swallowed, fear and excitement creating sparks in her eyes. He could almost see her heart beating out of her chest. "Yes. Yes!"

She nearly ran back to the bike.

"Okay, hold on happy-pants."

He strapped the helmets to the back rail, made sure his woman was secure against him, and set off.

He heard every breath, every cry, every exclamation. She squealed like a little girl and every time she buried her face in his neck he made another promise to keep her this happy. Always.

THE FLUSH HADN'T LEFT her cheeks even after they'd parked the bike in the garage and headed back into the house. He turned toward the kitchen but she pulled him up the stairs. Before catching his breath, she had stripped him down, crawled on top of him, and put him so far down her throat he was sure she had rearranged her anatomy.

If this was her reaction, he would happily reconsider his rule on having the bike to the city.

It was so hard to stop her, but he had to. He needed to be inside her. When he flipped their bodies and reached for the table on his side of the bed, she pulled him back to her.

He hovered, her legs spread so wide for him, the head of his cock so close he could feel the heat of her core. Goddamn.

"Connor." He snapped his eyes open. Something was happening on her face.

"Yes, love. I just need to-"

"Connor." Hell. His name from her lips. "Would you like to ride... without a helmet?"

It might as well have skipped two weeks to the Fourth of July because fireworks shot off in his head. His heads.

"Do you mean..."

"Yes. You know I'm protected. And clean. I haven't been with anyone since I've been in Virginia. And actually months before that, only ever with a condom-"

"Jenna."

She pulled her quivering lower lip under her teeth. "It's okay if you don't want to. I understand. Can't be too-"

He pushed the head of his cock into her and a throaty cry out of her. Her eyes locked on his as he lowered himself.

In the seventeen years since the last time he'd had his bare cock inside a woman, either female anatomy had significantly changed or the woman whose flesh was currently squeezing him to within an inch of his life was something altogether different.

"My God," he breathed into her mouth. "This is unbelievable."

"You are unbelievable. In all ways."

This transcended sex, as if all his senses sharpened and softened at the same time. He looked into her eyes, glistening, and nearly lost himself. "Can you feel the difference?"

She blinked and a small tear pushed across her temple. "Not so much down there. But a lot," she put her hand on her chest, "here."

The world ground to a halt. Everything became silent and still in Connor's mind, as if he had dropped into the deepest meditation. Without effort, his breath aligned to hers, the wave of his motion matched by her tuned response. His movements were smaller, her touch was lighter, their kisses softer. He lost track of where he ended and she began.

THEY MISSED DINNER. By the time they got downstairs, Lucas and Ramona were snuggled on the patio, looking out toward the water. Lucas kept his funny looks to himself, while Ramona, in comparison, had all sorts of non-verbal commentary. Connor clearly couldn't tell her off—in her condition—but he wished she wouldn't be so... Ramona.

After scavenging leftovers, which he couldn't imagine being any more delicious, he and Jenna joined them outside for the final remnants of the sunset. They sat silently. Something had happened in the bedroom that had nothing to do with sex and he wanted to talk to Jenna about it. Find out if she was feeling it, too. But he couldn't find a single word to describe it.

Could it be possible that he had fallen even more deeply in love with her? All those parts of her she was sure he would despise were like magnets that pulled him closer. It had never been that way with anyone else in his life. He didn't like bad, messy, or otherwise unruly behavior. He preferred the people around him to be orderly, predictable, and obedient.

Everything changed when she walked into his life, taking all his requirements and flipping them. He wanted everything she was—tender, wild, brilliant, fragile, powerful—to weave itself so deeply into him that there would be no more room for sickness and hurt and being so fucking alone.

As the sun dipped below the water line, leaving only a whisper of orange in the purple sky, the word he was looking for finally came. Forever.

"WHAT'S THE PLAN FOR TONIGHT?" Lucas asked, breaking the silence.

Ramona answered. "We were thinking of taking the boat out tomorrow, so we might need a grocery store run for supplies."

"The boat?" Jenna asked.

One more thing Connor had left out in his description of the getaway. "Yeah, we have a boat we take out on the lake. Spend the day out there, relaxing and swimming. We bring food and drinks. It's really fun."

She ran her palm over his chest, which, if the other couple weren't right there, would have caused him to throw her down on the floor and take her. "That does sound fun. Is there a store nearby?"

Lucas stood up after a glance at his watch. "Yeah. I can run down there. Baby, you want to come with me?"

Ramona shook her head, definitively. "All my rotundity is home for the evening. Sorry, honey. Why don't you go with Con?"

Jenna stood up. "Actually, I'd like to go. See what the town looks like."

Lucas put up his thumbs. "Excellent."

Connor curled his lip. Being away from Jenna was not part of his plan for the night. He glanced at his sister, trying to get comfortable on the seat. Maybe some time alone with her was a good idea.

Jenna dipped down to kiss him. "Can I get you anything special?"

She already had. "You know exactly what I want."

"I'll be back soon. Don't miss me too much."

Impossible.

CONNOR WAITED for his sister to return from her hundredth trip to the bathroom. He refrained from giving her shit because there were much more important things to discuss.

"How you feeling, Mo?"

"Mostly good. Sometimes terrible. I can't believe in six

more weeks a human being's gonna come sliding out of my parts."

He made a face as if he'd just witnessed a horror scene. "Whoa."

"Anyway, I know you're going to yell at me for what I said to Jenna. I'm sorry, okay? It was well-intended and poorly executed. I'm blaming baby Winnie."

"Nice. Blaming the baby." He scowled. "I just want to know why you approached her. Are you really worried?"

Ramona took her time in answering. "Maybe I am, Con. You've got your campaign and your heart in the same person's hands. It's so much. And you know how things can shift," she snapped her fingers, "like that."

"Not us, Mo. Jenna and I are solid. Like, more than solid. This relationship is only going one direction and it's not anywhere bad."

"Slow down, big brother. Lucas' mother has been saying that Jenna's going back to California after the election. What are you going to do then?"

His breath stuck. "That's just a misunderstanding. Aunt Olivia was being pushy and Jenna pushed back. That's all. She's committed to this. To me."

Even as the words were coming out of his mouth, he knew the extent of his assumptions. He'd heard what Jenna said about her life back home and made the leap that she wouldn't want to go back. Then he'd taken her professions of love and assumed that meant she was now all in. All her statements of disdain about being White-House ready had been forgotten.

"I'm going to ask you something, Con, and you have to promise to not get mad at me. I'm doing this to make sure you're protected, that's all."

Interesting timing on the idea of protection. "I wish you wouldn't, but I know that's not going to stop you."

"If it comes down to Jenna or the Senate and you have to choose one, will you be able to? Without spiraling? Without losing yourself again?"

He didn't attempt to open his mouth. The only answer he had wasn't going to make his sister happy. At all.

CHAPTER 30

One week to election day

Jenna hated being late. Connor did, too. And yet, there they were, watching the minutes tick by. Instead of being backstage, getting mentally prepared and mic'ed up for the final debate, they were still in the car, fighting.

"This is your last chance to show the people who you are. To stop coasting. Senator Macklin has been coming after you for weeks now. Your refusal to take it seriously is making you look weak and incompetent. All the things she's accusing you of."

"I'm not interested in a boxing match, Jenna. That's not the kind of politics I'm willing to play."

She dropped her head in her hands. This man was going to hand his opponent the win. And the reason formed the entirety of her worst nightmare.

"I'm telling you, if she comes after you, you have to put your hands up. Protect yourself and then punch back. That doesn't mean you fight dirty or you pummel her, but you must fight back."

He shook his head. "I'm not going to."

The closer they'd gotten to the election, the more frequently this strange behavior appeared. Connor had run out of fight. Or decided he didn't want it any more. And if he had admitted to either of those things, she would have supported him. But she knew he wanted it as badly as ever.

It was exactly what everyone had warned her about. He had gotten distracted and opted for the easy way. They were so happy together that he got confused. She could not let him smash his dreams to the ground. Her heart wanted to encourage him with tenderness and love, but that hadn't been working, either. He was like an impenetrable wall of steel.

"Connor, this is the kind of indulgent madness that wouldn't be appropriate even if you were ten or twenty points ahead. But you're not. You could just as easily lose this thing as win it. Is that what you want?"

He tipped his head and gave her a half shrug. As if they were discussing whether to have sushi or Italian for dinner. Holy hell.

Uncle Robert had insisted that she keep pushing. So had Ramona. Jenna needed to do something to light a fire underneath him. As much as she hated getting him mad, she was running out of ideas. "If Macklin was a man, do you think we'd be having this conversation about whether to hit back and what was or wasn't respectful?"

He paused, justifiably confused. "Now, you're being ridiculous."

"Let me answer for you. No, we wouldn't. We would be strategizing how to take him down, once and for all. We'd be plotting where and how to strike, how to use his own momentum against him, the spot to hit with the greatest impact. This idea you have of trying to protect her, maybe because she reminds you of your mother or something, is not chivalrous. It's the highest degree of chauvinism. She is fierce and she is strong and she is currently kicking your ass, all while you're holding out some deranged notion that she's delicate and needs your protection. You need to snap out of it, Connor. If you're really interested in being Senator, that is."

"Don't you dare-"

She exited the car without looking back. Whatever was going to come out of his mouth next wasn't going be any good for either of them. But maybe it would inspire something better than what he'd been delivering.

The past several months of the campaign had been equal parts bliss and struggle. Their relationship was as perfect as the campaign was terrible. Unseating an incumbent was not for the faint-hearted, and her superhero boyfriend suddenly decided to stop reaching. To be content instead of driven. He was going to lose.

She could have done a better job, been more clear about their future. Been more honest about her misgivings. They could've chosen to have a frank discussion instead of getting lost in how wonderful it felt to be together.

The AV team put their hands up when they saw her walk in without him.

"He's coming, guys. Just hold on."

"I'm ready to be mic-ed up," his voice boomed from behind her.

The two men flocked around him and starting weaving the wire around and under his suit.

She knew he was staring at her and finally gave in to meet his gaze. She stepped in front of him and began vigorously smoothing down the front of his suit, as if he was covered in lint. Maybe hoping it would slap some sense into him.

"I want you to know that I heard you, Jenna. I got it."

She was certain he hadn't. All the fire was gone from his eyes. "I hope so."

SHE PEEKED BEHIND THE CURTAIN. Full house. She wasn't the only one who understood the stakes of this debate.

He stood at the edge of the curtain, head down, breathing and tapping. Senator Macklin was introduced first and appeared from the other side of the stage to a rousing round of applause. She had been adored in Virginia for nearly twenty years. But she'd outlived her usefulness, and her scandals had started over-shadowing her accomplishments. It was time for new blood, new ideas, new energy. And the man next to her was exactly the one to do it. If he could just resurrect the fighter within him. He needed to be a tough guy, maybe for the first time in his whole life.

The applause began to die down as his introduction began. Jenna put both palms on his chest and looked him straight in the eye. "Go out there and do what you do best Connor Francisco Barrett. Lead."

He walked out on stage to the hoots and hollers of his fans. The bright spotlight illuminated the sheen of his suit, which he wore like a boss. If only he could feel as dominating as he looked.

Connor had nothing but respect for the Senator, which was apparent as he genuflected when he offered his hand. Like a gentleman addressing the fucking Queen. Jenna let out a curse so loud the stage-hands froze and stared.

AFTER NEARLY AN HOUR of vigorous debate, there was no clear winner. Connor had held his own, an improvement over the last debate, but what he needed was a decisive win. The only possibility turning around the direction of the election. With one week left, there was no time to dick around. He needed to deliver the deathblow, but all he had were compliments.

Exhaustion pulled her shoulders down into a slump. The fact that they had been so close made everything worse. If she'd never succumbed to her feelings for him, he would still be hungry, be striving, be pushing toward the goal that had defined most of his life.

And then Macklin pulled out her own weapon: the anti-Barrett sentiment coupled with Connor's relative inexperience. It worked every time. The crowd went wild as she kept repeating that all his family knew how to do was get rich. Working hard for the people of Virginia wasn't something they could ever do.

Jenna's entire body felt like it had been doused in gasoline and set on fire. She could hardly watch, and turned away. Connor would be smiling and nodding as if Macklin's statement deserved respect. He'd be waiting for the crowd to quiet, then he would make his logical, level-headed arguments that no one would hear because all they were feeling was the heat of Macklin's emotional outcry.

Then all went silent. She spun toward the stage in time to see Connor slipping off his suit jacket, and it knocked her so far off balance that she reached out and grabbed the nearest solid thing, which happened to be the burly arm of one of the stage-hands.

She gasped. "Sorry."

He lightly patted her hand and a smile filled his bearded face. "It's okay, Miss. Somethin' big's about to go down, looks like."

Her heart started beating in her throat as Connor undid

first one cuff, then the other. The audience stared open-mouthed, maybe wondering if they were going to be presented with a striptease. He stepped out from the behind the podium as he meticulously rolled one sleeve up to his elbow, then the other. Even Macklin stood speechless, eyes bugged out so far they threatened to fall out of her head.

"Let me tell you something about hard work. It's something I understand very well. You see, I had a famous family. I can't argue that. But it wasn't all big houses and silver spoons."

A titter floated across the crowd.

"You might have heard that my father died recently. For most of my life, he was very very ill with alcoholism. It made for a difficult childhood, as you might imagine. But it taught me self-reliance and how to recover from challenges that felt much bigger than I was. Because I know what that's like, how hard it can be, I ask that of you, my fellow Virginians, with full knowledge of what I'm asking.

"I know that recovery from economic depression takes work. I know that raising a new generation that is more literate, more technologically adept, more globally-minded, takes work. I know that solving our problems takes work. And it's not just for me to ask and you to do. I am rolling up my sleeves and ready to work with you and for you. I haven't been sitting in some tower making demands. You've seen me, in your towns, in your homes and businesses. Listening to what you have to say and doing something about it."

The silence hung for just a moment before exploding like a crashing wave.

Jenna gripped her new friend as if he was keeping her standing, but when he pulled his arm free to join in on the applause, she had to join him. Connor had gone in a direction she'd never seen. More personal, more casual, hell, even deconstructing the suit he was famous for. It made the entire middle of her body flip and flutter. This man deserved every vote in that room because, unlike the bullshit constantly spewed by Macklin, he actually meant what he was saying. He had been working his whole life to make things better.

The crowd stilled once again, in preparation for questions from the audience. Jenna stared at the sea of faces, wishing she could read their minds. It would've been great to be certain that Connor's rousing speech would make enough of a difference. She would've loved to be filled with the confidence that had flavored the campaign just a few months before. But, realistically, it could well not be enough.

The growing distance between Connor and his goal was all her fault and she was going to make it right.

Jenna pulled out her phone and stared at her shaking hand. Connor deserved this. She pressed the call button on a recent contact.

"Hi, it's me."

"Hello, dear. How is everything?"

"It's better. But not good enough, I'm afraid."

"Oh."

"I need your help." Her voice cracked.

"Yes, anything."

"I need you to fix this."

Only his breath filled the line for several moments. "Are you sure?"

"Yes. I don't need to know how or what. I just need you to do what we discussed."

"He must never know."

"Understood. Thank you, Uncle Robert."

CHAPTER 31

*T*his was not how election day was supposed to go.

Connor was supposed to wake up next to the love of his life, who'd be wearing nothing but the diamond on her left hand. Instead, the bed was empty and the ring still hidden in his sock drawer. She was supposed to help him pick out a suit, then fiddle with his tie a dozen times before being satisfied that it was straight. He'd watch her tuck all that beautiful hair away and have the same pang of sadness every time she did it. But it wouldn't last because she would turn to smile at him and everything in his world would be as it was supposed to be.

It had been three days since he'd heard her voice—other than the recording on her voicemail, which he'd heard about ten times every day. He'd confronted her about the leak that had basically incinerated his opponent's campaign, and she didn't try to deny it. He'd yelled at her. All those terrible things came out of his mouth, mostly because he didn't want to believe. And now, she wouldn't even talk to him.

He'd been in shock. He said the wrong things. He got way too angry, the thought that she believed he couldn't win it on his own like a vise grip to his heart. She had always been the one who believed in him the most, and that final move proved she didn't believe in him at all. He held on to the sliver of hope that maybe there was a different explanation. But he couldn't find out because she wouldn't talk to him.

Everything about it was doused in shame. Overpowering, soul-crushing shame. From the fact that she'd been forced to compromise herself, to do the thing that had so disgusted her, to the recognition that she didn't believe he could win otherwise. Add in his explosive anger when he'd confronted her, and it was as ugly as anything he'd ever created. Maybe even uglier than what used to be his worst secret.

The scandal had his uncle's fingerprints all over it, but Robert would never have taken those measures on his own. Connor didn't care that the information had been leaked. Macklin's string of boy-toys was the Hill's worst kept secret. So fucking what. Was that supposed to be in any way different than her male colleagues who'd gotten away with that kind of behavior since the beginning of time?

What kept a constant clench in his gut was that he'd forced Jenna to do it. Made her go dark just because he hadn't fought hard enough to win.

He'd known, from the moment his sister had asked him, that the choice between Jenna and being a senator was not a choice at all. She was everything. She was the only thing.

His body slumped onto the bed and shook. He was about to achieve a dream he'd had for twenty years. Twenty fucking years. The win was finally within reach. And it couldn't have left a more bitter taste in his mouth.

He had his own grenade that could be detonated at any time. It would so far outdo Macklin's dalliances that there would be no contest. He just couldn't tell if pulling that pin would bring Jenna closer or push her even further away.

He got to his feet. Maybe this was exactly the time for desperate measures. He tapped out a brief text. *I'm going to tell my secret. I'm sorry.*

He waited for the little bubbles to pop up, indicating she was composing a response, but nothing happened. He stared for a few more moments before sliding his phone in his pocket, at which point it rang. Thank God.

"Don't do anything. I'll be right there," she said. Then the line went dead.

He wore a path between his room and the front door. Desperately wanted to see her, but didn't want to look too anxious. But he *was* anxious. Nearly out of his mind. Fuck.

He unlocked the front door, walked to his room, then back out to the living room. Why was he playing games? This was Jenna. He'd never been closer to or more honest with another human being in his whole life. He sat on the couch, closed his eyes, and counted.

She ran into the house, bundled in sweats and a parka, hair piled on top of her head but flying everywhere.

He rose as if his body had come back to life. Her. There. In front of him, again. "Jenna..."

"You haven't done it yet, have you?"

It took a beat for him to understand. "No. You asked me to wait. I did."

She exhaled and dropped her hands to her knees as if she had sprinted to his house and was out of breath.

"Are you okay?"

"Yes. The car was stuck in traffic so I ran."

"You ran?"

"Yes. But that doesn't matter." She looked at him with pain scrawled across her face. "Connor, why would you do this? It's here, you realize. Everything you've always wanted. Why are you doing this?"

"You're right. Everything I've always wanted is here. In front of me."

She covered her face with both hands, head shaking and speech muffled. "No, no, no. You can't do this. Please don't do this."

In three steps he was around her, arms pulling her in. "I can't have this on your shoulders. What you had to do..."

She pulled away. Her whole face contorted into disbelief. "On my shoulders? What are you talking about?"

"I put you in a terrible situation. Then I yelled at you. I didn't mean what I said. I was just in shock. I'm so ashamed of what happened and I don't blame you for being mad. You had every right."

Her eyes flickered all over the room as if she was searching for something that made sense.

She stripped off her coat and he could have dropped to his knees that second. Draped over the perfection of her body was his frayed Georgetown sweatshirt she'd spent many mornings snuggling in.

"I'm not mad at you. I was, at first. Frustrated, actually. I wanted you to do what I had done. I wanted you to fight. Then I realized it was another thing I'd misunderstood. It's not for the candidate to do. It's a job for his people. And *I'm* your people."

He pushed a breath through his pursed lips. He had geared up for her anger, for her blame and judgment. But not for this. "Are you really saying you weren't mad at me? Then why did you disappear?"

"Because you were angry and I wanted you to be. I needed you to want it like you used to. Before me. Before us. I wanted to make up for stealing this from you and the only way I could think of was to get Uncle Robert's help. And to stay away from you."

It was his turn to feel the punch of disbelief. He'd been so certain he understood her motivation and her feelings. "So it wasn't about you not wanting to be with me? Of being embarrassed of me?"

"I don't understand where you would get any of this from. When have I ever been embarrassed of you?"

"You've never had to compromise yourself, what you believe in, for me. Until that day."

Somehow her body grew taller and more regal, the look on her face as serious as he'd ever seen it. "I don't know what you think happened, but you've gotten it completely wrong. I would do it again. Right now, without a second thought. I didn't lie, I didn't cheat, I didn't go after an innocent person. I just brought Macklin's game, the one she's been playing all along, right back to her. I made a move and I don't have a drop of regret about it."

Her words boomed through the room, sending him to sit. He'd gotten it as wrong as a person could get things. "You didn't steal anything from me."

"But you gave up. Why?"

As if someone had flipped the switch, turning on the lights in his dark mind, he began to see. They had completely mis-interpreted each other's actions. She thought she'd caused his shift in the campaign, he thought he'd disgusted her into leaving. But they were both trying to love each other. They just didn't know it.

He reached his hand to her, to join him on the couch. "My whole life I've had one goal. I went after it at the expense of my family, of my friends, of love. It never crossed my mind that something, anything, could be more important. Until you. I didn't lose sight of the goal, Jenna. I just got perspective. I know it must have been confusing to see the change in me, but it was a good thing. I finally became a three dimensional human being. My love for you made me more suited to lead. Not less."

"It looked like you were trying to lose. It made no sense to me. "

He had to be honest. "Maybe I was, to some degree."

Her face immediately went white, eyes filling. He didn't think his heart could break anymore, but he was wrong. Again. It seemed to be a new habit.

"Oh, Connor. It kills me to hear that."

He pulled her in closer. "We've had a crazy few months. My niece was born, Camille and Jackson got married, the campaign grew in intensity every day. Somehow, we never talked about what would happen afterward. Maybe we were both scared too address it." He certainly was. "So, if I didn't win, we'd have more time to decide. I'd have more flexibility."

She bowed her head, her chest rising and falling in a jagged rhythm. "Let's talk about it now."

"Yes." He thought about the small box in his room. This was not how he'd planned it. He was going to take her out after the debate but she'd been so mad at him. And it had gone downhill from there.

"But first, are you still thinking about confessing your secret?"

Her voice snapped him back to reality. "I don't want this hanging over me for my whole career. If I proactively address it, I can control the narrative. It can't ever be used against me."

He knew she couldn't argue that point.

"You're right. But it's not the right thing to do today. Let's work on it, craft the message, and do it deliberately. Not in reaction to what just happened. We can figure out how to cause the least amount of damage."

The first thing he noticed was the recognition that the

woman who made his heart skip also set his brain on fire. The second was her use of the word 'we' in terms of their future.

"I love you, Jenna. More than I knew it was possible to love someone. I want to be with you and I'm willing to do whatever it takes for that to happen."

She took that beautiful hand of hers and touched his cheek, so lightly he pressed into her to get more contact. "I'm not going anywhere, Connor."

He'd heard her say that before, but he needed more. "I'm going to ask for more specifics."

She smiled as if she knew he would. Which she probably did. "Of course, love."

"Does that mean in Virginia?"

"If that's where you are, that's where I'll be."

He almost groaned at the first explosion of his heart. But he had to keep going. "Does that mean with me in the Senate, if I win?"

"*When* you win. And yes. As far as your career takes you."

"Oh." He didn't try to swallow the adoration and relief and astonishment that burst through him. Instead, he pulled himself away from her and stood up. "I'll be right back."

CHAPTER 32

Inauguration Day

Jenna ambled through the large hall, each click of her heels echoing while she moved from table to table and fiddled with the decorations. The room was flawless, decorated in blue and silver, understated and breathtaking at the same time. Just like Connor.

She'd left the house early, prepared to make last minute changes or deal with a crisis or two, but there was nothing for her to do. He'd made it so hard to extract herself from his arms. When he wrapped himself around her and pressed his lips to her neck, she almost lost her resolve. She could have accepted his enticing invitation, as the event planner and caterer had done a great job.

Her hands trembled as she smoothed an unwrinkled, crisp, white tablecloth. A swirl of emotions kept her breath shallow and her heart beating faster than normal. Maybe the time she now had could help her mentally prepare for the day. To gather her thoughts. The peace and quiet would vanish as soon as the hundreds of guests arrived.

One year ago, almost to the day, she'd been standing in that same room in the Mellon Auditorium, feeling bitter, cynical, and drowning herself in tequila. Her life had become a series of messes that she'd grown less able to recover from. But she'd had no interest in walking away from that life— stewing in it seemed like just punishment for her ill deeds. It had taken the collective push from her brother, her parents, her best friend, and that wonderful man who'd stolen her heart, to force her to see another possibility. When it came down to it, though, she'd had to take the step herself. And she thanked heaven that she had.

Jenna shifted the oversized bowl of mini Twix bars over a couple inches, then back again. She grabbed a handful, realized she didn't have any pockets to place them, and dropped them back in the bowl. Connor's sole vice never ceased to bring a smile to her face.

The ding of her phone across the room pulled her from thoughts of sweet men and candy. Camille, now officially her sister-in-law, sent a text letting her know that she and Jackson were on their way with the rest of the family. Along with a stream of hearts and kissing emojis. Just like the first time, her entire family was going to be there, including Connor's new niece, Brie.

A sense of warmth rose from the center of her chest. Her life had gone from gritty to glorious in a matter of months. She'd never considered that she would find a man who could handle all of her. No one had ever come close. Some loved the bad girl, many loved the good girl, a few loved the boss. People couldn't reconcile driven Jenna with fuck-up Jenna. Hell, neither could she.

But all of it was true, and it had gotten harder and harder to keep tucking parts away. When Connor walked across that stage, a crack formed through her center. The spark of surprise, like waking up for the first time, had blossomed into the greatest thing that had ever happened in her life.

The most honest thing she could say about Connor Barrett was that he rescued her. He showed her how to be afraid and brave, how to be honest and strong, how to hold someone with such strength that they had no choice but to let themselves be known.

She adjusted the new ring on her finger, centering the large Princess-cut diamond. It gave her a jolt every time she remembered it was there. Connor had chosen it all on his own and couldn't have picked better. It was elegant and modern, engraved with My Golden Girl inside the band. Stunning, and as bright as her future.

They hadn't yet announced it, but they were going to get married in just a few months, while Congress was on recess and before she started her assignment at The Brookings Institution, the most influential think tank in the country. Some serious strings had been pulled to get her that position and she didn't mind one bit. That, combined with the time she spent teaching the kids at Ramona and Camille's children's center would keep her just busy enough. Never too busy for Connor, though. That promise was one of several they'd made to each other.

"Jenna!"

Ramona hurried in from the far entrance, infant strapped to the front of her body.

"Hey, Mo." They hugged as much as they could with baby Brie between them.

Ramona took Jenna's hand and looked around the room, brown eyes so much like her brother's, scanning every detail. She sighed. "Part of me still can't believe we're here. That he did it. My big dork of a brother. God, how can you stand it?"

She could hardly, either. "I know. I'm pinching myself all the time."

Ramona spun around, which caused Brie to make the most adorable yelp. "All because of you, Jenna. I'm so happy to have you in the family. Thank you. For everything, including not telling me off when I deserved it."

She returned Ramona's smile. "Why are you here so early?"

"I wanted to make sure you didn't need anything. Can I help?"

"I don't think there's anything to do. Other than celebrating."

"Oh, I sure am ready for that!" She looked down to the sweet face snuggled against her chest. "Aren't we BB?"

Jenna stroked the baby's fine gold hair. "Can I hold her?"

"Absolutely. BB loves her Auntie Jenna, doesn't she?"

It was amazing how Ramona, who had scared the shit out of Jenna on more than one occasion, was now dealing in pink bows and baby talk.

Jenna lifted Brie from the holder and held her tiny body in the crook of her arm. She took a huge sniff of baby smell and exhaled. It might have been incomprehensible that her life now had this much beauty in it.

LUCAS AND CONNOR entered minutes later, well before Jenna had had her fill of that sweet baby. She and Connor agreed they wanted to wait at least a year before kids, to have time for them as a couple, but something made her think they wouldn't last that long.

Lucas took his daughter from Jenna's arms, while Connor went in for a deep hug. "How's my beloved?"

"So fucking happy, it should be illegal," she said into his

delicious neck, which was impossibly, even better than baby smell. "How are you?"

"Double that."

He turned himself to face inside the tiny circle they'd made. "Before it all starts, and I get all wrapped up, I want to say something." He cleared his throat, emotion broaching that powerful face. "You three are everything to me. There's nothing good in my life that is not directly attributable to one or all of you. Thank you for everything. I'm going to do everything I can to make you proud."

"We're already proud, Con-man," Lucas said, eyes glistening. "Always have been."

"And now, I'm going to borrow my wife-to-be for a second."

It felt like a feather tickled along her entire spine whenever he said that, and she happily followed him to the front of the room.

"Senator Barrett, what can I do for you?"

He picked her up and whirled her around until she let out a squeal of delight. Even after her feet touched the ground, she held on to him as her head spun.

"Just that."

"Really? You just wanted to spin me around?"

"I wanted to hear you make that sound. It reminds me of... something." That face was all sexy smirk. "And also, I wanted to have a minute alone. You ran out of the house this morning as if you were on fire. Didn't even give me a chance to properly thank you."

"The first two times did the job quite well. And there will be plenty of opportunities in the future."

He held her face in his hands. "A lifetime's worth, to be exact."

When would this man stop making her swoon?

"I'm going to say something in my talk. About us. Just wanted to let you know."

"I think all of our guests already know about our engagement."

"Maybe. I'm going to mention it anyway. So that it's official and all."

She grinned. "Official. Got it."

He pulled her in closer. "I thought we could announce the date, too."

She chuckled. "Gosh, you just can't keep a secret."

"Clearly," he said with a sweet shrug.

"Considering we just decided last night, and our families don't even know yet, I think we should wait. We can announce it later, back at the house. You know people are going to freak out that we're giving them two months' notice. I bet everyone will think we're rushing because of a shotgun situation."

"I think I've exercised infinite patience. Every day we're not married is one day too long."

She couldn't have agreed more. "Soon, my love. For now, you're about to have a room full of adoring fans to greet."

THE ROOM BUSTLED with excitement as she and Connor made the rounds. His hands never left her back, her hand, or her hair—which she'd worn down for him—from the minute he made his grand entrance. They had only covered a fraction of the room when Uncle Robert moved to the small stage and spoke into the microphone. Everyone gathered round.

As she watched Connor walk to the podium, a distant memory flashed in front of her eyes. Instead of that statuesque man striding across the stage, she saw a little boy sporting a red cape and glasses too big for his face. He skipped around a backyard, arms stretched forward, promising to save the world. She'd hidden behind her father's leg, not quite ready to play with the big kids, but found that odd boy fascinating. She hadn't known the half of it.

He paused after his opening remarks, applause filling the room. He stretched out his arm to call her to his side.

"And here's the one who made it all happen. Who organized, cajoled, threatened, and encouraged me and our wonderful team of volunteers and staff members to run a campaign I'm proud to have been a part of. I think there are a lot of politicians out there who can learn a thing from this woman about what power looks like. Please welcome Ms. Jenevieve King."

The volume of sound in the room doubled as she walked across the platform.

He wrapped his arm around her and held up a hand, waiting until the room had quieted again. "I want to share something very important with you all. As the election approached, Jenna and I found ourselves at a crossroads. The original plan was that she would return home to California, to resume her life before I'd upended it to run my campaign."

Grumbles and boos filled the room.

"I realized I couldn't let that happen. So I offered her a new position."

An excited titter nearly drowned out his next words.

"One that included the word forever. And a very special ring."

The crowd erupted in near deafening applause, hoots, and hollers. He touched her cheek and leaned in for a kiss. Impossibly, the crowd grew even louder.

She looked up at him, beaming at her, waving at the hundreds who'd come to celebrate their victory. The roar of the crowd faded behind the lingering warmth of his lips on hers, the feel of his hand around her shoulders, and a spark of recognition.

As he slowly removed his black-rimmed glasses, and then smoothed his jet black hair back into place, she realized a few things:

1. Her aversion to grand adventures was completely gone.

2. The man who'd taken her completely by surprise had some striking similarities to Clark Kent.

3. She might well be White House-ready, after all.

DEAREST READER,

I HOPE you enjoyed Jenna's and Connor's remarkable love story. If you'd like to share your thoughts about the book with others, I'd be delighted for your review at your preferred book retailer or review site. Reviews support independent authors!

FOR ALL THE perks of being a cherished reader (which you are), and be the first to know about new releases, sign up to be part of the Smart & Sexy Reader Team. I regularly send out book bonuses, audio clips, playlists and other goodies to make the wild ride even more fun. Get on the list at http://bit.ly/PEKSignup.

IF YOU CAN'T WAIT to find out what happens next, flip the page to find an excerpt of Consenting Adults , the next book in the Friends & Lovers Series. Thank you again, and I hope to see you soon between the pages of my steamy love stories.

Pascale

Excerpt from CONSENTING ADULTS
Book Four of the Friends & Lovers Series

*N*o matter where Talia forced herself to look—at the dancing couples, the luxurious decor, any one of her many family members—her eyes kept landing on the most surprising guest in the room. Tyler Diamond was at her cousin's wedding. *The* Tyler Diamond.

She knew it was him. She'd been introduced and everything. But the man who'd shaken her hand and smiled bore no resemblance to the one always depicted in ironic t-shirts and messy hair. Real-life, three-dimensional Tyler Diamond, in the sexiest suit she'd ever seen, was all sorts of hotness. Square-jawed, broad-shouldered, bright-smiling, with thick dark hair and dreamy brown eyes. Too much gorgeousness. What the actual hell?

Then, he'd sat directly across from her at the table, making avoidance impossible. She had no idea why he was there. Was he friends with Jackson? Another member of the much-too-hot-for-my-own-good club? None of it made sense, including the fact that every time she looked in his direction, he was already staring at her. And *not* at the redhead on his arm causing all the other guys in the room to drool on their ties.

Talia willed herself to turn toward the next table, where several of her aunts and uncles sat, then to the next filled with an eclectic mix of very beautiful people. She wasn't a stranger to celebrity, but this group was strictly A-listers. Much too impressive to have her attention hijacked by a single man. But she couldn't look away for more than a few seconds.

Tyler gave her a wide-eyed smile. He hadn't even tried to conceal his shock when she'd told him she was part of the family. But that was no different than anyone else. Talia stood out in the Pemberton clan. Even with a Dutch brother and a Japanese brother—with matching stepmothers—Talia's particular set of features often made her feel like a spotlight followed her every move. And not always in a good way.

She still had relatives who didn't appreciate Percy Pemberton's foray far from their Southern gentility roots. Her father had assembled a mini United Nations of ex-wives and kids who brought a splash of color and spice to the previously all-white Pembertons. It might be fair to question the *whiteness* of an old plantation-owning family, but that wasn't something Talia felt motivated to investigate. The color of her skin was neither a project nor a burden.

Somehow, Percy's serial philandering hadn't alienated any of the women and children, and they stayed glued together like a stock photo for diversity. Her rag-taggle assortment of family was her version of normal, even if it came with consistent servings of odd looks and disapproval.

That awkwardness with some of her more distant relatives was why Talia had built a life in New York City, hundreds of miles away from the homestead in Virginia. No one cared about her exotic features and tapestry of a family there. The way she looked, a unique multi-racial blend, garnered a fair share of lurkers and trophy-seekers. It could well have been that Tyler's interest was more about collection than attraction. It was most likely she'd never find out.

Talia's date, Brandon, howled from the bar on the other side of the room, where he and her two brothers had begun a post-dinner drinking competition. He, with his impressive stature and ethnic ambiguity, could easily be confused for the third Pemberton brother. If she hadn't known that his parents were from the Caribbean, his combination of dark skin and light green eyes might have been difficult to understand. Like her brothers, he seemed to get more and more handsome over the years.

Just that morning, she'd worried if bringing him to the wedding had been a bad idea. She and Brandon had decades of history, from playing together as kids, through school, and moving to New York. There were moments, including this one, when she felt the tug between viewing him as a brother, a friend, or something more.

It would've been so easy to be with Brandon. He was already fully integrated into her family and clearly cared about her. If she ever decided she wanted him, in that way, he'd almost certainly reciprocate. But she could never sustain those feelings for more than a passing day or two. If she hadn't invited him, it might have been easier to-

She stopped herself from completing that thought. It wasn't as if Tyler was currently for the taking, anyhow. Those were the kinds of fantasies she wouldn't allow in her life. Like a silly crush on a rock star.

Talia glanced away from the ruckus around the bar and landed on the bustling dance floor. No surprise, Jackson had hired one of the most famous DJs in the business, the one whose name people who'd never been to a dance club still recognized. The music was off the hook, and people were having a great time. A particular hunky body continued to catch her eye.

Of course, Tyler Diamond could dance. Much better than someone who looked like him should be able to dance. His body was strong and lithe, and he definitely had rhythm. He reminded her of Justin Timberlake.

He did a spin and pointed his butt toward Kendra, who gave it a loud smack. Everyone around them burst out laughing, then copied the move. The guy was smooth as silk, but not in a *too cool for school* way. In a *I'm so cool I don't care what you think about my dorkiness* way. To top it off, he was a bloody genius. One of the smartest people on the planet, allegedly. If nothing else, that was enough to get her engine going, but he had the looks and the charm to back it up. Add in all that power, so solid it didn't need to be broadcast, and Talia was a goner.

Tyler would be her kryptonite. Good thing that was never going to happen. One look at his date made that clear. Kendra was another goddess in a room full of the pathologically gorgeous. Even if he wasn't acting like he was into her, the fact that she was his date made it clear what type of woman he chose.

Brandon, Perry, and her middle brother Jonah rushed the table and too many arms pulled her to standing, bumping her body toward the dance floor. Yeah, this song was hot. One of her favorites.

The crowd cleared just enough for them to enter into the fray. In seconds, she was lost in the pounding beat, the pleasure of movement wiping all her worries away. By the time things started to slow down, each of her brothers was well in the sights of some young things, which left her and Brandon alone. He stepped toward her and wrapped his arm around her waist. A chill bristled down her spine. A single slow dance should have been fine with her friend. But something about it felt far from fine.

She pulled back, putting a couple extra inches between their bodies.

"What's wrong?" he asked.

"I'm just so hot. After all that dancing."

Instead of responding, he brought his cheek to her temple. The movement put what was behind him directly into view, which happened to be Tyler Diamond's big brown eyes, fixed on her while his own date's head rested on his shoulder. He moved closer to Talia, and for just a moment, she could imagine the two people between them disappearing, and her being in Tyler's arms.

She dropped her head. What was happening to her?

"Are you sure you're all right?" Brandon's deep voice sounded directly into her ear.

"Yeah." She separated their bodies and fanned her face. "I think I need some water. I feel like I'm overheating."

As much as she could pretend that everything was fine, the look on Brandon's face confirmed otherwise.

TALIA TOOK three big gulps of water, put her glass down, and leaned against the bar, grateful for a small moment of stillness. A large set of hands wrapped around her waist, causing an unwelcome bristle. She pivoted, ready to scowl at Brandon, relieved to see her brother instead. "Hey, Jo. Why aren't you still on the dance floor? Those bridesmaids aren't going to seduce themselves, you know."

Jonah's angular face brightened into a neon smile. "I'm good, sis. I'm not trying to score tonight."

She turned to study him. Her brothers took the art of the pickup as seriously as a heart attack. "Is that so?"

"Yup. And you?" Her brother waggled his brows at her.

Talia finished the last of the water in her glass. "Me neither." Which was not the whole truth.

He cleared his throat and tipped his head toward the dance floor, where Brandon was doing 'the bump' with the bride. "There's always that guy..."

Talia sighed. "Not gonna happen. I wish everyone would stop-"

"But it could. You just have to figure out what you want."

How bad had things gotten that she was now getting

relationship advice from her younger brother? "Anyhoo, have you seen Dad? I've been looking for him all night."

Jonah shrugged. "I'd guess, on the search for wife number five? It's been a few years..."

Talia croaked out a disgusted cough. Unfortunately, her brother was probably right.

"Let's go check out the dessert room," he said, pulling her away from the bar. "I heard some women moaning in there."

She let herself be tugged along, laughing the whole way.

They didn't even bother to sit down, popping the bite-sized delicacies in their mouths and sharing their own moans as they grazed the numerous tables.

"Hey, who's that guy you keep staring at?" Jonah mumbled with a full mouth.

A chocolate truffle fell from her fingers onto the floor. "What?"

"You keep staring at that guy wearing the sick suit. I think he's with a redhead."

Talia took her time picking the chocolate morsel up off the floor. There was no fooling her brother. "Tyler Diamond. You know, the tech guy. And I'm not staring at him."

"Hmmmm," he answered while examining something sprinkled with gold dust. "If you say so."

Of course, it had to be at that moment Tyler walked into the room, and there was nothing she could do to stop herself from following his every step. He stopped at the first table and picked up a strawberry. She closed her eyes and exhaled before turning her attention back to her brother.

Jonah's ridiculous smile filled his entire face. "You were saying?"

She elbowed him in the ribs and they both burst out laughing.

The rumble of Tyler's deep voice pulled her to him, as if

he had her attention on a leash. "What's good on this table?" he asked.

She swallowed, but couldn't speak, her mind so busy with the only answer she could think of. *Me. I'm what you should be having on this table.*

"The gold balls are amazing. Definitely try those." Jonah came to the rescue. "Hey, I'm Jonah. Talia's brother."

Tyler matched Jonah's smile. "Awesome. I'm Tyler. Nice to meet you."

He pointed to the gold-dusted truffles. "These?"

Jonah nodded and Tyler picked one up. He could have been moving in slow motion. His fingers hovered in front of his beautiful lips before he separated them and slid the chocolate in. The muscles of his jaw rippled as he worked the truffle. A low pitched sound came from his closed mouth, pleasure sparkling in his eyes. Talia couldn't exhale enough to dissipate the heat building in her body.

Jonah popped another one in his mouth. "Good, right?"

"Yeah. I think they're filled with brandy. Wow." Tyler's eyes skipped to Talia. "Which one is your favorite?"

The one right in front of me. "Those tiny rum cakes on the first table. Crazy good."

A chorus of gasps announced the entrance of Tyler's date, leading a group of open-mouthed women. The statuesque redhead made a bee-line for him, while her pals scattered to the many tables covered in exquisite desserts.

She placed her palm on his chest. Talia could've sworn he flinched. Or maybe she just hoped he had.

"This room is unbelievable," his date said, her eyes beaming. "Like I've died and gone to chocolate heaven."

Tyler's face looked like having to smile was causing him pain. "Talia, this is Kendra."

"Nice to meet you," Talia said, but Kendra's attention had already flipped to the table.

"You too." She slipped her arm through Tyler's. "Which ones have you had, Ty? Tell me what's good."

Talia stepped back. Yes, this was the reality check she needed. Tyler Diamond was way outside her league. And taken. "Enjoy all these goodies," she said to Kendra's back and Tyler's confused face. She couldn't get out of that room fast enough.

The cool air outside was a welcome break. Talia lifted up the hem of her dress and strode away from that building as if it was on fire. Getting all twisted about Tyler Diamond and his rude girlfriend was a waste of time. Too bad she couldn't shake it.

She found her father on the veranda, admiring the sweeping view of the darkened vineyards and star-studded sky. His face lit up the moment he saw her. They walked toward a set of benches tucked under an enormous willow tree. Her fingers itched for her camera, or even her phone, but neither were available. This property was designed to be photographed.

He brushed a few leaves off the bench for her. "How's my cinnamon bun?"

She snuggled next to him and squeezed his hand. This was exactly what she needed. Her father might have been the most imperfect man she'd ever known, but he was a great father. And she loved him.

"I'm good, Daddy. Everything's going great." Sparing him the details of her latest upset was the least she could do.

"That dress is somethin'. That green color was designed for your skin. All those boys in there are nearly losin' their minds."

She bumped his leg with hers. "Stop it, Daddy."

"I'm serious. You're lookin' like a million bucks."

She ran her hand across the silky folds of the long skirt. The moment she'd seen the dress, she knew it would be perfect for Jackson's wedding. It was bright, bold, and demanded attention. She didn't mind.

"You still takin' those pictures?"

If he only knew how much her secret hobby had blown up. "Yes. But work has been so busy. After the car campaign, we got a rush of new clients. They keep announcing the death of the advertising business, but our company is booming."

He flashed her the trademark Pemberton smile, the one that set hearts on fire across five continents. Even in his sixties, her father was still a very handsome man. His blond hair had thinned, but covered most of his head. And those blue eyes could cut through metal. "I'm so proud of you, darlin'. Makes me feel like I didn't screw up so badly after all."

She dropped her head onto his shoulder. The night sky, spotted with more stars than she'd ever seen in the city, startled her. She'd nearly forgotten that she was across the country. The landscape could almost have been Virginia, where she'd grown up. The vast swatches of rolling green hills, the quiet sounds of the country, the smell of dirt and growth.

"How's your momma? Seen her lately?"

"She came to the city a couple months ago and we got to spend some time together. She's killing it in London. Has another show coming up. I think she might even have a slightly royal boyfriend."

His body shook under her as he laughed. "Ha! That Allegra... As talented as she is beautiful." He planted a soft kiss on the top of her head. "Just like you, dumplin'. But where's your royal boyfriend?"

She sat up and gave him a fake glare. "Don't start with me, Daddy."

He put up his hands in defense. "Arright, arright, arright. I'm just trying to get a sense of when I need to have my pennies all lined up for that big weddin' of yours."

"Dad, we all know the next person in this family to get married will certainly be you. And maybe Jonah after that. You can keep your pennies however you want them."

"Fine," he huffed. "But I don't want any surprises, hear me?"

She hadn't been surprised by a man in a really long time. "Don't worry. No surprises."

Talia closed her eyes, the sounds of the night sliding into the foreground, and the wedding festivities fading behind. She took a deep breath and relaxed into her father's arms again, enjoying his warmth against the dropping temperature.

She rarely missed this sense of family. Hers was so big and loud and smothering that getting away from them was the only way not to be overwhelmed. In that moment, surrounded by almost all of her relatives, at least on her father's side, she felt more grounded and connected than she had in months. She might have been an outlier, but her family had proven themselves, over and over, large enough to contain her. The one exception—the old woman who'd hated the fact that Talia existed—was long gone.

"Ya know, I heard there's some fancy cellar around here. Jonathan King invited us all down there for Cognac. What do you think? Should we go crash the gentlemen's party?"

"Aren't you supposed to *be* one of those gentlemen, Daddy?"

"Well..." his eyes filled with mischief. "I'm not sure anybody at this party still believes that to be true."

She laughed, hopeful. Another gentleman, one with a

surprisingly nice ass, might also be there. As she walked with her arm threaded through her father's, the possibility put a much more noticeable pep in her step than the growing chill of the night. She might not be able to have Tyler Diamond, but he was damn nice to look at. And talk to. And who knew what else.

＊

WANT to find out what happens next? CONSENTING ADULTS can be found at all major retailers.

ALSO BY PE KAVANAGH

FRIENDS & LOVERS SERIES

Collecting Secrets (Book One)

Coming Home (Book Two)

Claiming Power (Book Three)

Consenting Adults (Book Four)

ZODIAC MAGIC SERIES

Casting A Spell (Book One)

THE PRICE SERIES

The Price of Desire (Book One)

Sex, Money, and the Price of Truth (Book Two)

Available at your favorite online retailers.

ABOUT PE KAVANAGH

I believe that everything we experience exists as a story within us.

My journey as a writer includes the award-winning poem I penned at the ripe old age of seven, decades of hiding and doubt, and then finally... finally!... realizing that art needs to be shared. Storytelling is part of my heritage, even though I denied it for so long. The stories I created - true and imaginary - have saved me numerous times.

My characters come to me, like old friends excited to tell me what's new. They represent the world I see and the world I want to see.

More than anything, I care about recovery from life's setbacks... getting back on your feet after life has brought you to your knees... and my characters fight the hard fight for the lives they know are waiting for them.

I've drawn my inspiration from the many flavors of my life experience. Once a sad, shy girl, I've also been an MIT-trained engineer, biotech executive, professional dancer, yoga teacher and business owner, school founder, spiritual counselor, entrepreneur, and author.

And I own a magic wand that I'm certain will work one day.

When I'm not typing furiously trying to capture the stories that pour from me, you can find me loving my people to excess, globe-trotting to the next great adventure, and sporting bright red lips as a tango diva. And of course on my digital homes: pekavanagh.com and boldsoulcoaching.com.

www.ingramcontent.com/pod-product-compliance
Lightning Source LLC
Chambersburg PA
CBHW070741180626
46818CB00007B/2936